Goat on the Menu

An Anthology

Fast Twitch Writers Group

Goat on the Menu

First edition, March 2012

Forestville, Sydney, NSW 2087, Australia

www.fasttwitch.blogspot.com

Cover Photograph: Bruce Lyman

Cover Layout: Michael Henderson

ISBN 978-0-9806623-1-3

Production/publisher: www.lulu.com

Orders: www.lulu.com, www.amazon.com, www.fast-twitch.com

Contents

The What?

The Fast Twitch Writers Group is an eclectic group of, well, writers. Real writers that is, not aspiring ones! We meet once a month and aim to encourage each other to write. Indeed, when we started in 2008 some of us had never attempted any creative writing at all. Few were published. Nonetheless we have surprised ourselves with the range of material crafted in our first twelve months which was published in our first anthology titled "Black and White with Colour". Productivity has been a little slower since but has nonetheless resulted in this volume which carries a goat motif. Just because we can! Fans of our own work, we fancy this volume reflects an improvement in our writing and ideas. We know you are going to enjoy it - hopefully even more in the reading than we derived from the writing. Don't put it down until you are done.

The group consists of all ages (primary, junior school and high school students and some who can barely remember when they were in school. It is a great mix, who manage to inspire and encourage each other. Which is the main aim of a group after all. We hope you enjoy this delectable menu.

Contributors

Mary Arch ◆ Stephen Chan ◆ Ellen Cregan ◆ Gordon Crossin ◆ Chris Dunkley ◆ Dylan Dunkley ◆ Sonja Goernitz ◆ Michael Henderson ◆ Bruce Lyman ◆ Greg Sampson ◆ Matt White

Goats in Paradise

Mary Arch

S OME MEMORIES ARE as repulsive as the dead goat I stumbled on.

I have a midden of memory fragments. Some cut like shards of glass, some float off like fraying threads. Others are luminous and pure like the sea shells I have kept. I try and distil sense from each piece and sculpt a story but the pieces are so very strange to me. And yet they are mine.

A children's rhyme takes me back to that goat. The words are imprinted inside me but they are foreign and I understand them only in part:

> *Tong kali tong manis, bunga mawar di bawa lonjo lonjo*
> *Pleng pleng pleng, ular nampleng ketemu na si goronipopo, si*
> *goronipopo, si goronipopo...*

It is a clapping song. Like our pat-a-cake rhymes. Gladis shows me. We are both twelve but her hands are so little and brown slapping against mine. Her younger brother sings it too, running up the beach.

I am collecting shells; small conches with fat peachy, beige lips. My pockets are bulging with them. Some of the children huddle around following my every move, giggling behind their hands and whispering to each other in their dialect. I understand enough of what they say: of my sisters I am the ugly one. I have a high nose, like the mast of a ship, and glowing eyes. Like a 'pongkok'. I ask them what this new word is. They look away and shrug their shoulders.

The goat is washed up on the beach. Bloated, and wide-eyed, it rocks and shifts with each nudge of the waves. When I almost step on it my stomach lurches and my legs tingle with shock. The other children don't seem to notice. Its stiff legs are flipping back and forth with each wave and there is a swarm of flies in its mouth. I run up the beach as fast as I can; my heart hammering against my ribs.

Gladis' little sister, Lena, finds a small yellow cowrie and gives it to me. It is sun-warm in my hand. "Mata kambing," she says. Lena has a crooked arm. It looks like she has two left elbows. Perhaps it was broken and never set again. I ask her if it hurts. She smiles. Maybe she doesn't understand me. We take the shells home and Lena shows me with her crooked arm how to throw ten of these 'goat's eye' cowries onto the concrete floor of our house and pick them up one by one in between the bounce of an old tennis ball.

As we play, other children climb up to the windows to catch a glimpse of my sisters and me. "Belanda, belanda!" they whisper to each other. They have only seen 'belanda' in the movies. The house is dark with the collage of their small brown bodies pressed against every window space. I want to shut the wooden shutters in their faces.

Some would say this is an island paradise. But in spite of its wild beauty there is a heaviness here. Some might blame the pressing heat or the parasitic smell of copra. But really it is a kind of darkness. It has settled its smothering weight over me. I can barely take a breath.

It makes me so tired all day and awake all night. It makes me detest food. Especially sago and fish head soup. Sago is like tasteless jellyfish. I try and swallow it in small amounts so as not to gag on it. The soup contributes some flavour to it but I avoid the fish head with its boiled eye staring up at me. For dessert there is ripe papaya. I cannot stand its sickly smell. Instead of eating or doing my lessons I lie on my bed. I get thinner and thinner, yet feel heavier and heavier.

My head bows when I walk. Such is the weight of this cloud. I do not see the hills or the sea; only the limestone ground and my big white feet.

There are goats apparently untended all over the town. They clamber over the rocky paths, perpetually searching for things to eat. At dusk barefooted boys chase the skittish animals back to their respective pens, swatting their haunches with sticks. Even though the goats wander at their leisure through the day, it is an illusion of freedom. I hear their desperate, mournful bleats.

I am an ugly, lonely, giantess whose eyes glow like a demon's.

The children teach me to play a game with a stick and a rock. We play it in the schoolyard next to our house. It is like softball but I don't understand the rules very well. They laugh at me each time I get 'out'. My father has explained to me in the past that they are not laughing to be cruel but to relieve the tension. But I don't care. I start screaming my frustration in English. Rage pours out of me. They stare at the ground and mumble between themselves. My face is red hot. My throat is sore. I walk away before they see the tears spill down my cheeks.

My family is invited to visit a smaller island. On the beach we are brought green coconuts from the trees that grow along the water's edge. These are cut open with machetes and we drink the sweet liquid inside and then the soft sweet flesh is scooped out for us to eat. It melts in my mouth.

That night we are invited to dance with the people of the village. In a circle we dance, two steps forward, one step back, around and around to their acapella songs. They sing in harmonies all night, I can hear them long after I have been sent to bed: "Hela, hela rotane, rotane, tifa jawa, jawae babunyi, rotan, rotan sudah putus, sudah putus, ujung dua, dua bakudapae...." They sing and dance until dawn.

In the morning I am taken out in a dugout canoe by some of the island children. The ocean water is almost still. From a distance it is an aqua colour but up close it is like looking into a glass of fresh water. The sea bed is powdery white and it is impossible to see how deep the water is. On the sand below I can see brightly coloured sea stars. The children dive down in their clothes and bring up the stars to show me. And then I dive down too. The water temperature is so perfect I feel nothing. Time stops. I am in another world. It is breathtaking. For a moment the dark weight is lifted and I am free.

Back in the town there is the homeless man. He is lying on one of the school's concrete verandahs. The children have told me that he is 'gila'. They said he was in the navy and that he is grieving his wife and children. I wonder if they have died or if they have abandoned him. His head is shaved and he is naked except for a pair of grey underpants. Every part of his body is muscular like an athlete. He has a scar that extends from his forehead right around to the back of his skull. He mutters and laughs to himself but other times he shouts in anger. Sometimes we hear him sing songs in perfect English. Sometimes he sleeps in the shed next to our house.

One day I visit Vera. She is ten years old. Her house is behind the school. Her mother squats on a stone in their dusty yard with Vera sitting between her knees. She is finding the nits in Vera's hair and they make a satisfying 'crunch' sound when she crushes them between her fingernails.

I think Vera's older sister, Kekek must be sleeping. She often sleeps all day. Vera is holding Kekek's baby in her lap but the baby is squirming. I pick her up and put her on my hip. We find a stick to play with.

I listen to Vera and her mother talk about what happened last night. Across the road a young woman was out the back of her house washing herself when she was hacked to death with a machete. They think it was her lover. They think she had cheated on him. They are amazed that anyone would go outside at night to bathe. What with all the 'pongkok' around.

A man comes asking for Kekek. He wears good shoes and has shiny slicked back hair. He does not remove his fancy sunglasses to speak to Kekek's mother. I am surprised. That is considered to be bad manners. Vera's mother calls Kekek. She walks out in a tight dress and high shoes. Painted lips and eyebrows. She wears a lot of gold for someone who lives in a house with a dirt floor. Vera tells me Kekek works at the hotel down near the boat dock. She is a 'hostess'.

There is another house, it is much smaller than the other houses and it has a pig pen out the back. A 'dukun' lives there with his wife and older son, Jonny. Sometimes they slaughter a pig at four in the morning. We hear it squealing. A few hours later Jonny comes to sell us the fresh meat slung on a pole he carries across his shoulders.

Gladis has told me that this 'dukun' heals people who are sick and helps women who come to him with their unwanted pregnancies. She explains that if the women don't have any money he asks them for other 'favours'. I wonder what his wife thinks of this.

There are two young girls from a nearby island who live with us and do our cooking and cleaning. One has curly hair and she laughs a lot. Her name is Eyam. The other one has straight hair. She has lost one of her front teeth and is very shy about smiling.

One day Eyam goes to see the 'dukun'. She comes back and lies on her bed and before long is moaning in pain. We can hear her loud cries from the room where we are doing our lessons. The other girl comes running to say that Eyam has eaten some moth balls to kill herself. My mother takes Eyam to the hospital. Eyam is four months pregnant.

When Eyam comes home she tells me that while she was at the hospital her baby slipped out into her hands while she was squatting on the toilet. The baby comes home with her in a small box which my mother buries under the custard apple tree in the backyard.

One night an ugly sound like thunder fills the air all around. My bed shakes under me and the wardrobe slides across the floor. It is an earth tremor. But it does not stop me.

Almost every night I wake long before dawn and slip out of the house. I walk and walk all over the town. For some reason I am not afraid of anything; not the dark, not the earth tremors, the machete killer, the homeless man, the dukun or the pongkok. I just want to walk. My parents do not understand. They forbid me from leaving the house in the dark but I don't listen. So each time I disobey them they forbid me from playing with my friends during the day. For weeks I don't see my friends. I don't care. I keep walking. Night after night.

During the daylight hours I lie exhausted on my bed unable to do my school lessons. One day the lethargy gives way to a headache so severe I think my head is going to split open. After a few days my neck becomes stiff and then my tongue is paralysed. I feel agitated and want to pace. When my mother realises that I can no longer speak she takes me to the hospital. We do not have a car. Public transport is our only option. We sit in the back of a small open van with other people coming back from the market. I feel strangely euphoric. My mother thinks I might have meningitis.

It is dark when we arrive at the hospital. I am slipping in and out of consciousness; vaguely aware of nurses whispering and taking my blood pressure. The Chinese doctor examines me and diagnoses cerebral malaria. It is serious. The fluid around my brain is inflamed. For the next few days I am so sleepy I hardly notice the large injections I am given; doses of Fanzidar.

When I am released from hospital I am too weak to walk and thinner than ever. For days I shake like I have Parkinson's disease. In the mornings my father carries me to sit by a window. I watch the children play outside. I am aware that I came close to dying. But for some reason I have been delivered. The darkness cannot have me.

Silence

Ellen Cregan

Silence from ceiling to floor
A beautiful ceremony
Bring people together
With smiles on each of their faces
They go home and end the day
Together forever

Silence from ceiling to floor
A stand filled with judging faces
Twice for some
Three times for one
About to decide the future
Of a man they have never met

Silence from ceiling to floor
A beautiful ceremony
Sending people apart
With frowns on their faces
You will forever be in my heart
Together forever

Meet the Parents

Dylan Dunkley

S HADOWS QUIVERED ON the wall as the candle flickered, then fizzled to nothing. I had been sitting in that seat for six hours straight. I was completely motionless, staring at a photograph of my late wife. Her name was Emily Cotchet and she had blonde hair and blue eyes. To me, she was the most beautiful girl in the whole world. We got married four years ago. I met her in high school and we started dating near the beginning of year ten. We married late March right after we finished high school. I couldn't stop staring at the photograph, thinking about how I would never see her face again, never hear her laugh, never see her smile. I had twelve candles lit around the table. Three of them had already gone out. Emily had died just the night before from cancer. As I sat, mourning her death, I remembered her, all the things we did and all the emotions we shared. There was one memory in particular that stood out from the rest.

It was halfway through the second term of year eleven and I was standing in my bedroom staring at myself in the mirror like it was the first time I had ever seen myself. I was wearing a black tuxedo with a white shirt, which acted as a good background for my red tie. I heard three firm knocks on my bedroom door.

"Yes?" I called.

The door slowly opened and I saw my mother standing in the doorway looking at me with a huge smile and her eyes welled up with tears.

"You look very handsome, but you really must hurry up or you will be late for your first dinner with Emily's parents. You don't want to make a bad first impression," she said, obviously holding back the happy tears.

"Don't worry mum," I replied. "I'm nearly finished."

She walked over to me and started doing mum things like fixing up my shirt; then she licked her fingers and started fixing up my hair.

"Stop that," I said as I pushed her hand away from my hair. "I'm not six."

She stood staring, the tears welling up even more.

"It seems only yesterday you were running around the backyard in your underpants chasing the dog," she said.

I finished putting on my shoes and socks and sprayed on some deodorant. I walked over to mum and put my hands on her shoulders.

"I have to go mum, so please step out of the doorway," I said, in the nicest way I could.

She gave me a huge hug and whispered in my ear, "Make a good impression."

"Don't worry mum, I will," I whispered back.

Two minutes later I climbed into my 1978 VW bug. It was an old thing that I got when I got my L's in January the previous year, but it had served my dad well before me and so far, it had not let me down. As she spluttered to a start, I headed towards Emily's house. Before I knew it I was standing in front of her front door trying to think of things I could talk about and how to greet them. I rang the doorbell and within twenty seconds I heard footsteps heading closer to the front door. My heart pounded, stronger and stronger with every step I heard, until finally the front door was opened, and there standing at the front door was Emily. She was dressed in a beautiful, glittery red dress with black high heels on.

"You're late," she said.

"I'm sorry," I said as I leaned in and gave her a hug and a kiss on the cheek. "I was making sure I was presentable. So, what do you think?"

"I think you look, very handsome," she replied. "But your fly's undone."

I immediately grabbed for the zipper to zip it up but I found the zipper was already done up. I glared at Emily.

"I'm trying to make you loosen up, Steve. This is going to be fun, they'll love you," she said, trying to comfort me.

"Well stop it, you're making me even more nervous," I replied.

"Is that Steve?" said a voice that came from what seemed to be the lounge room.

"Yes Dad," Emily replied.

Within five minutes we were all sitting around the dinner table, except Emily's mum who was putting the food on the table. She started with putting a large roast chicken on the table followed with bowls of potatoes and vegetables. She ended with a couple of bottles of soft drink. We said grace, then began piling the food onto our plates. An awkward silence lingered.

"This chicken is fantastic Mrs C.," I said, eager to break the silence.

"Thank you, Stephen," she replied.

The lingering awkward silence began to arise again until Emily's dad broke it.

"So, Steve, were you born in Aus.?" Mr Cotchet asked.

"Yes, but I was not born here in Sydney. I was actually born in the country," I replied.

The questions started piling on and everybody grew less nervous of each other. By the end of the night we were all laughing and I was sure that I had made a good impression.

Three hours later, we had all finished eating and it was about time for me to head home. I said my goodbyes and headed towards the front door. I opened the front door and Emily jumped me from behind.

"I just wanted to say," she said. "You did a good job."

"Thanks," I replied.

I found myself staring at the photograph laughing at the memories that had returned to me.

I took a deep breath and stood up. I turned the photograph face down and blew out the remaining candles that were still alight. The room went black.

Jus ad bellum

Bruce Lyman

J UST WAR IS well, just war. We want to argue some wars are
fought in the name of justice and that some are not. We want
to distinguish defensive from offensive, arguing a defensive war
is more just than an offensive one. Consequently we tangle
ourselves up in debates about defensive wars that take the
offence, quickly realising such a basis is a weak foundation for
the argument. So we fall back on justice defined from the
perspective of the aggressor, from that of the target, from that of
victor to that of the vanquished, and sometimes even from that
of the rescued. In the end most debate occurs between those
who have the luxury of standing on the sidelines. They bray
about the injustice of the justice, and their media feeds sound and
emotional visual bites that the masses parrot and recite.

No one ever asks Jacob, the person relieved of his misery, a
relief ironically brought about by the war imposed on his
country. Those on the sideline focus only on the fact that a large
nation invaded a smaller nation. Never mind that Jacob's family
now contained no men of marriageable age, an elderly patriarch
whose sightless eyes weep a steady pus and whose final vision
had fed a broken mind images of a dull orange branding fork.
The young boys of the family compound melt back into the

palms when a foreign vehicle approaches. For years these vehicles had belonged to the secret police. Then they belonged to strangely clad men who watched carefully, handed out sweets, said little, then vanished again. After a period the secret police returned, this time shooting and raping and pillaging their way through the remote compound, screaming obscenities about their proximity to the border and questioning their loyalty to the supreme leader. The old man had his eyes cooked in his head in this period. Jacob had taken to carrying a grenade after his single brief but bloody encounter with these men. They would die with him if they attempted to arrest or interview him again.

By the time the strangely wrapped men with their sandy hair and dark glasses returned, with vague promises of help, and the secret police had faded away, there was no compound to speak of. Jacob had taken to living in a cave near the river. His small herd of goats were his primary source of food and were his safety alarm as well. A goat's curiosity took them into folds in the ground and holes in the rock invisible to Jacob. Places where enemies might hide. And if a stranger approached the flighty skip of each goat set their neck bells clanging and jangling, putting Jacob on his mettle, with plenty of warning time.

The horizon had flashed and burned for many days and nights. Jacob had watched from the old compound, along with the young boys. Every rolling clumping bang was met by a groan of terror from the old man, resting under his palm. He refused to enter a closed room ever since the police had released their blind prisoner to find his own way back home. Jacob shivered. His country was being attacked. His people killed. By whom he was not sure but he suspected the sandy haired men in their sunglasses had something to do with it. They did not hurt anyone that he could see (everyone had noticed that when they were in the area the secret police vanished) but they were strangers in his land. Infidels no less, on sacred ground, men who did not observe prayers and fasting or holy days. Jacob's stomach churned in horror – what if they took control and proved worse masters than their own secret police?

The flickering horizon faltered and petered out after a week. The occasional crump and faint dusty flash hinted at continuing battle. Jacob moved up the river following his goats which quietly moved as a loose mob from palm shade to palm shadow, nosing along creek beds and across sandy ridges as they sought out the greenest green. Jacob wandered behind them, carefully watching where he put his feet. Not lest he triggered anything but because sometimes in this ancient dust fossils might be found or even more valuable, a clay shard with strange symbols that university people would get very excited about. And pay a little money.

The jangle of bells caught his ear. Then the silence grabbed his attention. He ran to the top of the crest. His goats were looking at something, paused in their foraging. A culvert under a dusty road. The kids skipped around but the nannies turned their heads as if in puzzlement. Jacob felt for his grenade and crept forward until he could see into the plastic pipe. One of those sandy haired men was curled up asleep, his rucksack partly blocking the culvert from view. His body rose and fell in breathing sleep, his rifle beside him together with his spare ammunition clips. An infidel making war against his home? Perhaps. Perhaps not. He could not be sure. Jacob primed his grenade, dropped it into the culvert and sprang away. His goats followed. The stifled crack of the grenade was followed by drifting smoke silence. He whistled up his goats who gamboled into a mob around him. "It's just war," he said to his matriarchal nanny who merely bleated her roundup call for the kids to fall in. Jacob followed her up the creek. "I need to find another grenade," he thought. "Just in case."

The Soldier

Chris Dunkley

TIME SEEMED TO have stopped. His mouth, frozen open, emitted a scream that would never come. His eyes, a deep blue, locked with mine. I couldn't hear the calls and shouts of those around me. The only thing I saw was his dead frozen face and my blood-covered hand. Slowly, ever so slowly, the surrounding sounds seeped into my head and the man in front of me collapsed, his eyes now a milky white. I turned to find another man, identical to the one I had just killed. Without thinking, my hand shot out, burying deep into his stomach.

My sight shifted and all of a sudden I was looking through his eyes, seeing my blank, emotionless face and my forearm protruding from this man's stomach. I watched myself pull my arm out, turn and punch the chest of another man. I was helpless, watching myself go from man to man, tearing heads off, hearts out, and breaking spines with my bare hands. I hear a gunshot, then darkness falls, like the curtain at the end of a play. The last thing I remember seeing was when I first killed someone. I was six.

It was the end of a bad week, and he pushed the wrong buttons. I lunged at him, my hand disappearing into his stomach. I gripped his spine and pulled, giving me a satisfying crack. I heard the door close and looked up. My dad walked out just as my uncle's body hit the ground, his old eyes blind to the light of day. Dad froze, looking from my uncle's body to my bloody hand and back again. Then my mum walked out and I knew I was in trouble. She took one glance at the body and screamed. She turned and ran inside, presumably going for the phone. Dad ran to the hose and dragged it to me, trying to wash the blood from my hand. I didn't flinch when the ice cold water hit my skin, I was locked in a trance, staring at the hole in my uncle's stomach, only just making out the shape of his spine. I stayed in that trance for the next few days, my eyes constantly staring into space, my mouth never uttering a word.

I woke up in a white room with cables attached to my body. All around me were strange men wearing white cloaks. I heard the scratching of pen on paper. Rolling my head towards the sound, I found myself looking into the dark eyes of an old, grey-headed man. The man smiled and put the pen and clipboard down. He stood up and called to the other men, gesturing towards me. There was a flurry of activity and I heard several clipboards hit the ground as everyone crowded around my bed. One of them asked my name. I tried to answer but no sound came from my open mouth. One of the other men fiddled around with a dial on one of the many machines attached to me. I felt a slight, but distinct electric jolt. This time, the old man asked my name, his voice sounding kind and passionate. "John Vale, I think," I managed to mumble, as darkness once again fell upon me.

I could hear beeping, some rapid, some like a song tempo. My vision slowly returned as my eyes peeled themselves open. There's only a nurse and the old man in here this time. I blinked, trying to clear my fuzzy vision. The old man saw me and smiled, holding up a picture. "The 1920 war, killed thousands. I was part of that war, you know, a sniper, the best in our battalion. They used to call me 'One-Shot', well that was until I was shot in the eye. I may only be able to see half as much, but I'm still just as alive as when I first shot a gun." I leaned over, intrigued by the picture.

There were four men, each standing to attention with rifles at their sides. "That one's me," the old man pointed to the young man at the end. He had short straight hair, a defined jaw, and an average nose. 'One-Shot' was on his shirt, 'Skipper' was on the man next to him, 'Radar' on the man at the other end, and I couldn't quite make out the name on the other man's shirt. I pointed to the man whose name I couldn't quite read.

"That's Roger, but we all called him Dodger. You see, no matter how many battles we got into, he always came out unscathed. I don't know how he did it, but he did. Anyway, we won the war and each of us," indicating the four in the picture, "came home with three medals each." Just then the nurse walked in with lunch, or at least I think it was lunch. I had lost track of time looking at the picture and listening to the old man. "Ah, dinner, better leave you to your food then. I'll be back in the morning to see how you're going."

I looked down at the plate lying across my legs, mashed potato, some liquid stuff, and apple juice. After eating the mashed potato, I placed the tray on the table next to my bed and lay back down. Staring at the ceiling, I tried to remember what happened. The last thing I remember was watching myself kill people through the eyes of another man. Try as I might, I couldn't remember what happened next.

"He's alive, barely." Pain, extreme pain, exploded through my body. I couldn't see anything, but from the sounds of things I'm glad I couldn't. "He's been hit in the chest and I can't find the bullet." "He should be fine. He's stopped bleeding and the wound has already begun to heal," the medic, I assume. I tried to open my eyes, but was rewarded with a blurry world through a millimetre wide gap. The medic, seeing my movement, leaned back and grabbed what looks like a bag. I feel a slight prick in my arm, then darkness.

I opened my eyes and was greeted by the warm sunshine coming in through the window. Looking to my bedside, I see the old man sitting in his chair, looking the same as the first time I saw him. "Morning." My voice is croaky, but still there. The old man jumped a little, probably surprised at hearing my voice.

"Morning John. How are you feeling?"

"Better, still a bit groggy though." I reached over and grabbed the glass of water sitting on the bedside table, hoping to wash out the dry feeling in my throat.

"You may feel that way for a few more days, but it will go away eventually. You took a serious blow, a blow that would have killed any normal person. When the medics found you, your blood had already clotted, and the wound was already starting to heal. You're a lucky one, I can say that much." The old man's face suddenly became distant, as though he was recalling a distant memory, possibly of his own time in the war. I lay there and let him think for a while, content with trying to remember as much about what happened that I could.

"Excuse me sir, but can you tell me what happened to me, I can't seem to remember."

"I'm sorry but I don't know any more than you do. No-one would say anything, they just brought you in here and told the doctors to fix you up as fast as they could, looks to me like they did a pretty good job." I looked down at my chest and studied the scar that spread from the centre of my chest. The scar twisted and turned, working its way from the centre of my chest, to either side of my torso. I suddenly noticed that there weren't any wires hanging off me. Suddenly, I had the urge to stand up and walk around. Lifting the sheets off my legs, I swung myself out of the bed and onto the floor. My feet hit the cold floor with a soft thud. I walked around for a bit, getting the blood flowing back through my legs and around the muscles.

Just then the nurse walked in. She looked at me and smiled, saying that I was free to leave whenever I felt like it, and my stuff was in a bag under my bed. I thanked her and grabbed my bag, looking over my shoulder at the old man, still staring into the distance. I shook my head and headed into the bathroom to get changed. When I walked out, the old man was once again sitting down, but this time he wasn't doing anything. I smiled and walked out the door, asking the nurse at the desk to say goodbye to the old man for me when he woke up.

A Little Bit of Duck

Bruce Lyman

I heard the phrase "A little bit of duck" on JJJ one morning and it caught my ear. I wrote the words down as a title on a blank piece of paper and the story materialised some time later as part of an exercise aimed at telling a story with dialogue.

"**G**ET YER BUM down."

"Shhh, you'll scare them away."

"Don't say 'Shhh' you idiot, it carries further than if you just told me to shut up. Shut up and get yer bum down."

"Wot's yer problem with me bum?"

"I can't see where they are. Blimey, do I have to explain everything?"

"Haha, yep, you sure do. Here, do I look fat in these."

"Shhh."

"I thought you said don't say 'Shhh' you will scare the buggers off."

"They won't be there the way we are going. Heck if we were sneaking up on the Japs up the Kokoda old General Tojo would have shot us five times over by now and gone home for 'is dinner."

"Admiral. And he wasn't in New Guinea."

"Whataya mean 'Admiral'? Is that a warning signal or summink?"

"Cor I am soaring with turkeys tonight. No you idiot, Tojo was an Admiral, not a General."

"Now you need to get yer bum down 'coz you are talking right out of it. An Admiral makes ships that shoots at other ships. He does not run around in the jungle. There are no ships in the jungle to shoot at."

"Only cretins like you. I never said he was in the jungle. Heck, it's too hard. Just shutup will you?"

"You're the one making the noise. I was just crawling along here minding my own business when you told me to put my bum down. Which it is by the way."

"Duck!"

"Where?"

"No, get down, someone is on the bike track."

"Could have told me sooner. Flip it's cold out here. Could have warned me it would be wet."

"Whatya expect, we aren't shopping for dinner down at Timmy's Kitchen."

"Well, you said it would be a walk in the park. Here I am crawling through long grass. And I don't think it is a park. Unless it's a national one. More like the bottom end of my grandma's orchard which was always full of long wet grass."

"You are a complete cretin. A walk in the park means...shhhh."

"What's up?"

"Those walkers have stopped. They're looking in our direction."

"Where?"

"Here, you dickhead."

"They can't see us. It is way too dark. They would need to be eating heaps of carrots to see us over here. Germans did that you know."

"Did what?"

"Eat carrots."

"What for?"

"So they could see the Raffie chappies heading in their general direction at night."

"You're a pillick. Why I'm crawling 'round here with you escapes me."

"Nah, it's true. Scientific fact. Where are they by the way?"

"If you put yer bum down like I asked I could see. Thanks. They're walking away. But they don't seem too sure. Let's stay here a minute."

"Get real, it's cold. As soon as they are out of sight, I am off. What are we hiding for anyway?"

"So we don't get caught."

"But we haven't done anything yet."

"Not yet. But when someone hears something unusual and sees your fat white arse galloping through the bush they might put two and two together."

"And get what?"

"Well let's see, that a complete cretin was out here poaching for starters."

"Who? Me! Nice mate you are. Besides, my arse is not white."

"Now that you mention it, from here you're absolutely right. Black hole of Calcutta actually."

"Haha, very funny, let's get a wriggle on. What's the Black Hole of Calcutta?"

"The big vacant space in front of me."

"No, come on. Seriously."

"Dunno mate. Some old prison I think. Full of poxy diseases and filthy water and lots of Indians. Bit like your place actually after a night on the curry."

"No Indians around my place mate!"

"Really? Coulda fooled me with all that vindaloo you knock back. Here, shuttup a second. Where the hell are we?"

"No idea. Just crawling along in the park. Hey, we never did sort out if we were in a national park."

"Never mind that, where the heck are we? I don't want any houses too close you know. And the university is just over that creek. Don't need any smart alec boffin swot heads hearing us. Be just like them to hear something at three in the morning."

"I think the lake is just over there, through those trees."

"Alright, let's get over there pronto. We need to ..."

"Holy snapping mackerel. Ya coulda warned me you were going to let that thing off."

"Shuddup, shuddup. Stop your shouting."

"What? Can't hear you!"

"Get down, get down. Stop jumping around. O Lord, we're gunna be sprung!"

"Wot?"

"Shuddup!"

"Get your hand off my face. Here, and mind where you are pointing that thing. That was a hell of a flash. Did you see the sparks?"

"Keep it down, will ya?"

"Wot?"

"Get off me, get off. You have flipped - first you try and shoot me, then you try and root me."

"For crying out loud, will you shut up? Didn't mean for that to happen."

"I still can't hear you."

"Jesus wept. And his Mother. Here, follow me. We need to get out of here in case someone heard that. Or can hear you."

" 'ang on, what about the ducks?"

"Forget the ducks, if we get caught here the cops will string us up. And I don't want to explain to the old man what happened to his precious Mossberg. I can't begin to think what he'll do if he finds out we have it."

"What's a Mossberg?"

"The gun, the er…never mind, let's go."

"The gun is named Mossberg?"

"No you cretin it's… ahh never mind. Let's just get out of here."

"Nah, quick, let me just see if you got a duck. We came all this way…"

"No, it was accidental. I wasn't aiming at anything, …hey, psssttt, where are you?"

"Shhhh, back in a sec."

"You idiot, we'll get caught."

"Stop yer stage whisper. It's bloody loud."

"I thought you said you couldn't hear anything…. What are you splashing around for you cretin? Where the heck are you? C'mon get out of there will you? Oi, what the heck is that… stop laughing will you."

"It's a duck, whaddya think it is?"

"You mean I hit something?"

"Other than the creek bank. Yeah, looks like it. Now let's get out of here."

"Been saying that a while ya moron…now what are we gunna do with that?"

"The duck?"

"No, the Ferrari we just stole. Who's the moron? Of course the duck."

"Sorry Dad."

"Sorry Mr Jamieson, won't never happen again."

"You bet your life it won't. What I'm doing bailing you guys out of the station at two in the morning is beyond me. Should have locked you both up and had the coppers throw away the key."

"Sorry."

"Explain to me again why you are down here."

"We was going for a walk."

"A walk."

"Yeah, a walk."

"What, with a bird?"

"Ah, yeah, ah, kinda. Yeah, yeah, a bird."

"What were you walking a girl down in this God-forsaken place – nah better not answer that. She must be as thick as you two. But here, you haven't answered the question of the duck feathers all over you."

"They were in the wet grass and got stuck to us."

"The copper said that too – reckon he believed that story of yours?"

"Yeah, of course. It's the truth."

"All right that's enough. Shut up the pair of you. When you think up a decent story, talk to me. Until then I don't want to hear a peep from either of you. For at least a week."

"Yes Dad."

"Yes Mr Jamieson."

"Mr Jamieson."

"Yeah."

Bruce Lyman

"What's a Mossberg?"

Ah, Spring

Greg Sampson

I KNEW IT was going to be a great day the moment I woke up. I could just feel it. There is always something in the air in early spring; it is my favourite time of the year. The sun was already warm when I got up and went to kitchen to get my morning coffee. The smell coming from the window that opened on to the back deck was wonderful. Jasmine blooming mixed with gardenia perfume was a heady mix for me. Ah Spring.

The light breeze rustled through the leaves and danced on face and arms, as I sat on the deck drinking. As usual a pair of rainbow lorikeets came flying in for their breakfast. I had their apple with me already and reached up to put it in the feeder. That quietened them down. They say the lorikeets all look the same. That may be true, but if you listen closely you can tell the difference, and I know it was always the same pair that came each morning to share this time with me.

I could sit here all day, ah spring, but there were things to be done. After I dressed, I picked up my back pack and cane from beside the front door and left to face the day. As I tapped my way along the footpath the sun on my face was amazing. Yep, it was a great day. Ah Spring.

Goats

Matt White

O NE EXPERIENCE I had with goats was when I was a kid and I was out at my dad's cousin's farm with my family. My uncle was giving the goats their medicine and I was roaming around the small paddock searching for a young goat to pat.

The rest of my family were getting the goats prepped for their medicine. My dad was filming the whole thing, so he didn't do anything to help.

Even my mum got in on the action of grabbing a goat and sitting down and talking to it. My uncle was the one to grab the goat and tip it on its back in this contraption so my big brother could give the goat its medicine.

Meanwhile I managed to get hold of the goat I was chasing and gave it a big pat.

Clinker Bill

Bruce Lyman

B ILL WAS FORTY-THREE years old when he shaved his legs for the first time. It had never crossed his mind to do this. Ever. Not that he had any aversion to the concept. In his school days he had a couple of triathlete friends who went into the whole body waxing thing and he understood why. Until now he had felt no impulse to do it himself which was odd, for Bill was a tactile sort of fellow, enjoying the feel of the sun on his skin, or the rush of rock foamed water massaging him as he tumbled through rapids to the pool below. As a boy his early excursions into his sexuality had nothing to do with either sex but a curiosity about the sensations created by the elements. The evening he started on his legs he had been reminiscing about those boyhood summer days when he lay barely buried, naked under hot sand, only his head exposed. The remembrance made him tingle and he wondered that it had been decades since he had done anything like it.

Those summer days were running and climbing days. Long days of shooting and hiking and exploring. The outdoors toned and tempered his fit young body and he once admired his flexed legs and arms, watching the muscle sculpt his skin. So there was a slight feeling of shock as he stared at his newly shaved legs. A healthy white sheen through the suds should not have surprised him. "Haven't been in the sun for years," he mused. The familiar childhood spots and scars were still there. What shocked him was not the colour but no matter how much he flexed, his legs would not sculpt. It was a loss that jolted him and which he mourned.

The loss still nagged him weeks later as he leaped two steps a time up the escalator to the street, on his way to the bank. True he could not run like he once did but he was fit. Surely he was. The sun had dropped but the sky was luminescent ink blue and throwing diamond glints of light up the street in one of those rare moments which warm the sandstone and which photographers, caught outdoors without their cameras, lament. Bill strode along Castlereagh Street, stepping around dark suits rushing home when the bright reds, yellows and blues of a brilliant handbag, artfully perched beside casually discarded high heels, in the same colourful and intricate pattern, caught his eye.

"If I was a girl I would buy those," he thought and in the same half step wondered why it was that he couldn't do just that. He rued he could not walk up the street with the handbag. It appealed to his love of irreverent yet harmonious colour. The sky darkened, the crowds pressed in and he hurried away. Besides, Albert who monitored the gas flow into the flue and checked furnace humidity and moisture levels would somehow find out he owned a handbag. That was his answer to "why not?"

The pressing crowds took his mind off the handbag, and he was weighed down by the thought that he looked no different to

all these other burdened people. Bill trailed a half balding middle
aged man in a dark suit who limped along under his own
extraordinary weight. His disposition already bordering on glum,
he now felt dark and moody. I am being taken where I don't
want to go and becoming someone I don't want to be. Van
Morrison broke into his head and Brown Eyed Girl pulled him
even lower.

> *Hey where did we go,*
> *Days when the rains came*
> *Down in the hollow,*
> *Playin' a new game,*
> *Laughing and a running hey, hey*
> *Skipping and a jumping*
> *In the misty morning fog with*
> *Our hearts a thumpin' and you*
> *My brown eyed girl,*
> *You my brown eyed girl*

He signed the documents and stepped back into the street.
Her lips were luscious and the long tangled hair fell carelessly
over her face. Tips of teeth barely visible, and an upturned,
inviting chin. Bill knew it was the advertiser's art, the powerful
language of sex being used in this oversized poster to sell …? He
wasn't sure exactly, since he had moved past so quickly, but his
peripheral vision had been caught by the sexual invitation. He
knew he had been suckered but did not blame the advertiser or
the model. He was conscious of a sensuousness that eluded him.
A line of lip, a shine of cheek, a glisten of sweat that he would

never taste or touch or smell. A loss discovered in the shaving and emphasised now in everything he saw. In the poster. By the Chinese couple French kissing behind the raised boot of their BMW in Haymarket. In the shampoo advertising in every hair salon. By the gorgeous models leaving at the end of the day from David Jones, a giggling cluster he was forced to step around. He put his head down and ploughed on, suddenly conscious of the stubble catching on the cloth of his trousers.

In the dark evening Bill slowed as he made his way to the train. The bank had knocked the stuffing out of him. Heck, what was he doing there at all? He should be back in the cement factory doing his thing. But an inheritance is an inheritance and needed looking after properly. It required his full attention and that was what he was giving it. Bill, now the sole recipient of a large injection of unencumbered funds, was suddenly more aware of life than he had been since he was a ten year old boy living in the bush where skinny dipping was a summer and autumn pleasure and no one cared if you liked flowers.

Albert worked the gas, while Bill supervised the clinker production in the rotating kiln that ground all day and all night. It was a good, tight team of bloke's blokes. Men who knew what they wanted and were sure of themselves. Or at least that was what they wanted everyone to think. Bill imagined that was the case with them all. And perhaps they thought that of him. He couldn't tell. Not really the sort of thing you discussed over the sandwich box was it? He turned his head to the rumbling roar of the turning kiln that made the clinker that made the cement that made the city that hemmed him in and wondered if it was all worth the worry.

The inheritance sat in the bank for three years. His bankers pleaded with Bill to invest in their funds but Bill feared that once he could not see it only the bankers would. So he left it where it was and read the three line statement that arrived in the mail every month to torment him with possibilities. He took flights of fancy to Morocco. Andra Pradesh. Tibet. Rio plagued his dreams. Themes of colour and light and texture linked them all. Early one clear morning in late autumn, with the sky starting to lighten in the pre-dawn silver darkness he became vaguely aware of a new passenger boarding the bus at the stop after his. He guessed she was in her mid to late thirties but it was hard to tell in the shadows of the morning. He was engrossed in his newspaper – but not so much that he did not notice her fashion sense. Over the next few days she sat closer and closer and she seemed to get clearer and clearer. Always smartly dressed. Soon he was waiting for her to get on, his paper unopened until he had seen what high heels and suit she was wearing that day. Hair neatly done. There was something of the 1940s about her clothes. Her skirt, of fine wool, came to the knee and her wide lapelled jacket was tied in the middle with a wide and brightly coloured sash. Only her hair suggested a more modern time.

On Wednesday morning Bill was startled to see her walk onto the bus with the purse he had admired in Castlereagh Street all those years ago. Somehow the purse was clear and brilliant, and in noticing it she also came into sharp focus. She unnerved him as she walked the length of the bus and took the seat beside him. He couldn't help himself and leaned to her, ever so slightly.

"That is an amazing collection of colour. I saw it in a store in the city and considered purchasing it."

"For yourself?" Her smile was gentle and Bill, normally inclined to defence, took no offence.

"Yes," he whispered. "For myself."

"I am glad you didn't. There was only one and I was so glad I was able to buy it."

Bill laughed. "I think it probably looks better in your hands than it would in mine. Chaps at work would think I had gone completely barmy if I turned up with one of these."

"Not the sort of thing I would take to work Bill. They wouldn't appreciate it."

"You are so right." He leaned back in his seat and briefly contemplated a scene of derision and abuse. Startled he lurched forward and started to open his mouth.

"It's okay, your name is on your lunch box. Or is it really your lunch box? Maybe Bill is someone else."

He relaxed back into the seat. "No, that is me alright. Tell me, did you buy the heels in the matching patterns?" He found himself looking into her face as he asked and the fine patterns of her green eyes and the careful black shading of her lashes caught his breath. She was going to accuse of him of being too forward. Any moment now.

It was her time to laugh. "You ask the question as if you will be disappointed if I said that I did. And if I did buy them you might be worried they were the only pair left as well."

Bill felt a sharp twist in his gut and only responded with a nervous giggle. How well she knew him. He shook his head. "No, shoes would not be for me. Not to wear at least," he added hurriedly. "But I did fall in love with the lines and the curves and colour. Not unlike…" He paused, embarrassed. He had nearly put his foot in it completely, and they had only travelled three stops together.

"Not unlike this suit? On me?"

"No…no…no. Nothing like that." Bill was appalled. How could she know? How could she be so forward? He shifted awkwardly towards the window.

"It's okay Bill. I am happy for you to tell me what you think. I don't think you could ever offend me. I like these lines myself. Classic aren't they?"

Bill nodded. This was going way too far and way too fast. He gazed out the window and there was an awkward silence for the next stop or two. Bill was conscious of a strong flower perfume, the scent of early freesias or daphne carried on crisp, cool, morning air. But the fresh glory of the freesia did not completely obscure the faint acid of damp clothes, as if they had sat in the clothes basket too long before being put out to dry.

Suddenly she was patting his knee. "See you tomorrow Bill. Let's see if you like the lines and curves of tomorrow's outfit." She laughed and lurched to the front of the braking bus, demounted and was gone. Bill quickly looked around but no one seemed to be paying any attention.

Soon Bill's day never started without the smell of flowers and the beautiful line of a knee length skirt as she came into view at the stairs of the bus. She was working in a government office she could not tell him about. Bill could care less. Here was someone who understood all the things he loved about fashion and colour. But it was more than that. He shared whispered family secrets with her and they laughed at childhood remembrances together. She told him about the life at school and at work though he often wondered that she never spoke about her family. They laughed and joked and giggled at each other's secrets. Passengers looked strangely at them, especially at Bill. He sometimes suspected they were alarmed at their frolicking laughter and noise. They never frowned at her, only scolded him with their eyes. No doubt they felt he should be more restrained, what with his grey hair and dull overalls. But he felt like a boy again and cared less about what others thought. He whispered his delight at the skinny dipping escapades as a child and his secret desire to capture that carelessness again. She clapped her hands and laughed and said she knew exactly what he meant.

The morning she did not arrive on the bus was the morning after Bill had been told he was to be made redundant. Maybe he could take that trip to Morocco. Something in his heart told him he could not. He wanted to ask her. Would she travel with him perhaps? A trip on his own now seemed empty and pointless. But she was not at her usual stop. Alarmed, he got off at her stop in the city and walked into the art deco building in Martin Place where she had said she worked.

"Are you trying to have a joke sir? No one by that name has worked here for years. But have a look at the plaque in the foyer. If you are not pulling my leg it may just be of assistance."

Puzzled, and quite a bit worried Bill made down the stairs to the foyer and found a loving memory engraved stone calling to mind a certain Jean Hathaway who had, to the deep regret of her colleagues (who missed her so), been killed in a tragic bus accident on 14 September 1944. Her faded, embedded picture was bounded by Australian flags and blooms of wattle. It was her alright, in her stylish wide lapelled jacket. It took Bill the whole day to walk home. He could not face getting on the bus and he never went near work. Albert had been right all along. She was too good to believe. "You have been inventing her," he would laugh as Bill recounted her witty conversation. His whispering and talking and giggling had been to empty air as far as his fellow passengers were concerned. What appalling things they must have overheard. And seen.

Police found Bill in his bath. Shaved leg hair floated in the grimy suds and cold grey water – which hid the pooled blood that had leaked from his body two days earlier. The iPod still hummed away on repeat. As they made to lift him from the drained bath the ambulance officers gently removed his earphones. The tinny strains of Brown Eyed Girl caught their ears.

> *Do you remember when we used to sing,*
> *Sha la la la la la la la la la la te da.*

Billy

Gordon Crossin

WHEN I WAS very young my Dad owned a small farm. On an open grassy patch, he heard his neighbour's goat Billy was too ornery to be kept anywhere else. He needed room. One day, Billy ate all the grass as far as his rope would allow. My Dad enlisted to help the neighbour to move Billy to a greener patch. Whilst the neighbour distracted Billy, my Dad ran in and dug up the stake, but as soon as the stake pulled free, Billy bolted, dragging Dad face-first into the mud. Just as Dad got to his feet, the neighbour ran past, saying, "All yours, Jim!" My Dad was completely unsuspecting when Billy, at full belt, butted him in the crotch. Dad tried to crawl away as Billy kept butting him in the butt. Dad managed to make it to a nice grassy patch near the dam where Billy lost interest. As my Dad drew the stake into the ground, Billy showed his appreciation by kicking dirt into Dad's face. As my Dad limped away, he realised he'd dropped his wallet ... which was now in Billy's mouth, getting chewed. Billy didn't like the wallet much and spat it into the dam.

Tamar's Kid Goat

Moses

ABOUT THAT TIME, Judah separated from his brothers and hooked up with a man in Adullam named Hirah. While there, Judah met the daughter of a Canaanite named Shua. He married her, they went to bed, she became pregnant and had a son named Er. She got pregnant again and had a son named Onan. She had still another son; she named this one Shelah. They were living at Kezib when she had him. Judah got a wife for Er, his firstborn. Her name was Tamar. But Judah's firstborn, Er, grievously offended God and God took his life.

So Judah told Onan, "Go and sleep with your brother's widow; it's the duty of a brother-in-law to keep your brother's line alive." But Onan knew that the child wouldn't be his, so whenever he slept with his brother's widow he spilled his semen on the ground so he wouldn't produce a child for his brother. God was much offended by what he did and also took his life.

So Judah stepped in and told his daughter-in-law Tamar, "Live as a widow at home with your father until my son Shelah grows up." He was worried that Shelah would also end up dead, just like his brothers. So Tamar went to live with her father.

Time passed. Judah's wife, Shua's daughter, died. When the time of mourning was over, Judah with his friend Hirah of

Adullam went to Timnah for the sheep shearing. Tamar was told, "Your father-in-law has gone to Timnah to shear his sheep." She took off her widow's clothes, put on a veil to disguise herself, and sat at the entrance to Enaim which is on the road to Timnah. She realized by now that even though Shelah was grown up, she wasn't going to be married to him.

Judah saw her and assumed she was a prostitute since she had veiled her face. He left the road and went over to her. He said, "Let me sleep with you." He had no idea that she was his daughter-in-law.

She said, "What will you pay me?"

"I'll send you," he said, "a kid goat from the flock."

She said, "Not unless you give me a pledge until you send it."

"So what would you want in the way of a pledge?"

She said, "Your personal seal-and-cord and the staff you carry."

He handed them over to her and slept with her. And she got pregnant.

She then left and went home. She removed her veil and put her widow's clothes back on.

Judah sent the kid goat by his friend from Adullam to recover the pledge from the woman. But he couldn't find her. He asked the men of that place, "Where's the prostitute that used to sit by the road here near Enaim?"

They said, "There's never been a prostitute here."

He went back to Judah and said, "I couldn't find her. The men there said there never has been a prostitute there." Judah said, "Let her have it then. If we keep looking, everyone will be poking fun at us. I kept my part of the bargain – I sent the kid goat but you couldn't find her."

Three months or so later, Judah was told, "Your daughter-in-law has been playing the whore – and now she's a pregnant whore." Judah yelled, "Get her out here. Burn her up!" As they brought her out, she sent a message to her father-in-law, "I'm pregnant by the man who owns these things. Identify them, please. Who's the owner of the seal-and-cord and the staff?"

Judah saw they were his. He said, "She's in the right; I'm in the wrong – I wouldn't let her marry my son Shelah." He never slept with her again.

When her time came to give birth, it turned out that there were twins in her womb. As she was giving birth, one put his hand out; the midwife tied a red thread on his hand, saying, "This one came first." But then he pulled it back and his brother came out. She said, "Oh! A breakout!" So she named him Perez (Breakout). Then his brother came out with the red thread on his hand. They named him Zerah (Bright).

(Genesis 38, The Message)

Not Alone in the Outback

Sonja Goernitz

I WAS SO depressed in Sydney I felt like killing myself. In tears I called my friend Bruce Lyman, CEO of a software company and administrator at the Frenchs Forest Baptist Church, on a Sunday night. He offered me to come along onto a trip with 14 teenagers into the outback in South Australia. Bruce had mentioned South Australia to me a few times, raved about it when he came back and would like to live there (a hunter's dream). This time I decided to come along. It'd only cost about $10 for the food for one week (!) and about $100 per person for the petrol. Yes, we were driving. In a convoy, connected with CB on channel 20. We stayed on a 40,000-acre sheep and cattle farm, which is run by an elderly lady (76), and helped with the cactus killing and renovating of the shearers' quarters. We city people learned a lot.

There were five responsible adults in our group: Bruce, Rodney Dunkley (the two made a good team, at the end of the trip even their body language mimicked), Bruce's son Dannie (25), Bruce's daughter's partner Harry (26) and I – though I did not feel very responsible. I felt as if I was one of the teenagers actually. On the backseat of the 4WD I asked the tall bodybuilder Shannon his age. 19. "Oh, I'm double your age." I'm not used to this. I'm not used to the action at all. I work from home, have my gentle meditation music on, candles and an oil burner with rose scent. Here I was with a bunch of teenagers and things seemed to be changing all the time. A few days on, Bruce's brother Frank and his family joined us. Bruce leads gently, Frank more directly. Both are ex-military, worked in intelligence.

We were not really comfortable. In the first night I wore two pairs of socks, leggings, pants, a t-shirt, a woollen jumper, a sweat-shirt, a woollen jacket and a woollen beanie in my sleeping bag. I was still cold. We were five women/girls in one room, two younger ones sleeping on the floor. The bed was hard. I felt better the next night because Rod gave me an extra minus-five sleeping bag and a doona. At night I had to go to the long-drops twice or three times. Terrible, but the stars on the way back were rewarding. We rarely showered (though we did use up the water supply), men didn't shave; women didn't wear make-up, we covered greasy hair with hats, caps and beanies. At this time of year there are not many flies. That was different when the group was here last time in November. Then it was hot too.

Miss Joy Betty has lived on this farm all her life. She was born in a hospital nearby and a photo in The Stock Journal in 1938 shows her as a three-year old by herself on a horse, mustering sheep. Miss Betty is mainly dealing with men. Women do not like her so much. Miss Betty said she likes the solitude, and mentioned one can be very lonely in the city. True. Her husband Ron died seven years ago. He had cancer. They were married for about fifty years, shared the love for the land, did their work together and enjoyed to laugh. Miss Betty said that when something went really wrong Ron cracked a joke and broke out in laughter.

Last year in July Miss Betty was attacked by an escaped prisoner who was on the run. When she got away and called the police, he shot himself dead in her house. The police arrived and she was about to clean up the mess. The police officers said, "We have people for doing this." It seemed as if she didn't mind. She had cleaned up worse before.

We saw sheep being shorn, sheep being killed, lambs' tails being cut off – hang on, killed? Yes. Frank cut the throat of the first sheep. We city people stood around the pen and watched it happen. Death comes in minutes. The blood looks like red paint. The windpipe is about two centimetres in diameter. Surprising how quickly a cuddly sheep can look like meat in a shop. Bruce killed the second sheep, a tad faster, also breaking its neck and holding the muzzle shut. These brothers grew up in a farming community and knew what they were doing. Education. We now understand and appreciate it more where the meat comes from. On this trip, six kangaroos were shot – not for fun, but for dinner. Their flesh was so fresh it was still twitching before cooking. Goats are a pest here and at times they end up in the stew too.

One night two sheep shearers arrived: the cousins Robert and Chuck with their two dogs, Arnie (after Schwarzenegger) and Turbo (so young, he still learns his name). They joined Bruce and me after dusk at the fire place. Keith, Dan and Scott arrived the next day. Enthusiastically Robert explained the work of the three bend-over men "on the board", shearing the sheep, his role as the sweeper, clearing the ground from wool and dirt, and Chuck's role "at the table", sorting the wool into clean and stained bits. There is sheep poo everywhere but that doesn't matter as long as it doesn't get into the to-be-shipped wool, because that could leave a stain, like a red sock in a white wash. Shearers earn $2.50 per sheep. If they shear too many sheep in one day, the tax rises to fifty per cent per sheep; the men are less stressed, so are the sheep.

Our main mission was killing cacti. The Government of South Australia partly sponsored and supported our trip because we volunteered to kill cactus. Cactus is a problem because the spikes get stuck in the sheep's wool and shearers get the spikes into their hands. The value of land also depends on the cacti on it. Like other detrimental species, the cactus is not native. Left alone it builds a proud presence and you can see plenty of large ones on the neighbour's land, who could not sell his property. Bruce organised us in pairs, walking across the country in a strategic line. Objective: find cactus, stab a hole into each leaf with a screw driver, then insert the blue liquid poison from a long metal stick, which is connected to the flat poison container to be carried on one's back. A dead cactus looks white and is fallen apart. Result: 261 cacti die.

Another mission was renovating the shearers' quarters: Frank had just arrived and within an hour gained an overview and a plan what needs to be done. All furniture out! It reminded me of an Aboriginal community with the furniture outside – I know that's different. Walls were cemented, windows fixed, undercoats applied; walls, windows, doors and chimneys painted; gutters emptied. Frank said they are good children but they need someone who leads them. By themselves they tend to hang out. Miss Betty was delighted, "Many hands make light work." At the end of our trip, Bruce reported after dinner to Miss Betty at the table what we had done and winked that we kept a mental list of the things that still need to be done, so we are happy to come back. Lately Bruce came here every two months, also by himself for some space from the city – one does not miss the mobile, emails, radio, TV, Internet etc.

On this trip, I asked myself how I fit into society. In this micro-community people naturally took on roles, such as hunting, cooking, cleaning. I took about 1,000 photos and people asked me to take their pictures. Photographer? I wrote 71 pages into my diary. Writer? I write this article. Journalist? My mood went from a minus one (on a scale from minus five, depressed, to plus five, happy, with zero being neutral) to plus three or four when Frank showed me how to ride the red quad bike and asked me to transport back a large metal ring to put around the camp fire. He kept calling me "Sophie". I did not correct him. It reminded me of a scary tape I listened to as a teenager, in which the male hero calls a woman, Sophie, and she gives him quick and accurate information, hence the hero can function better. I like that. Sophie. Researcher? I do work for Peter FitzSimons. He advised me, "Write a biography about a person you like and respect." Miss Betty!

In a convoy of six cars (Bruce's green V8 up front and five white cars behind us), it took us 16.5 hours to drive back to Sydney in one go, with a few short stops in between. I wanted to stay in the outback, not face my life in Sydney again, where I have to find a flatmate and a part-time job, where you walk on concrete, don't see horizons and feel surrounded by glass and steel. On the long roads Bruce and I blasted the stereo and kept listening to the Rolling Stones' song Heartbreaker again and again. I said, "Australia can't be big enough for this."

Firestick

Matt White

O NE DAY I was walking down the street and saw dark black clouds to the west. I thought, "This is going to be a big storm when it hits – I'd better get home soon before that storm comes." About two kilometres away from home I checked to the west and saw that the storm was travelling faster than I first thought. Five hundred metres away from home I looked up and the storm was right overhead. I started running towards my house and suddenly a big flash of light, immediately accompanied by a big crack of thunder, surrounded me and I felt a massive burning pain shoot down my spine. Then everything went black.

When I awoke I was thinking, "Where the heck am I?"

I looked around and realised I was in a hospital. I couldn't work out how I had got there. Later a nurse came in.

"How are you feeling today Monty?"

"A little sore, but okay," I replied.

The nurse attended to my back and arm, both of which felt like they were on fire. When she finished she said, "Okay Monty, I'll be back later to give you a sponge bath. If you need anything just push this button."

Some time had gone by and I was thinking, "Does anyone know where I am and what happened?" Later I heard footsteps coming towards my room and when they got to my room my mate Steve appeared.

"How are feeling buddy?"

"Okay I think."

Steve laughed. "I saw you running past my house and then saw you get struck by lightning. I rang the ambulance and went to the hospital with you to see if you were okay."

After Steve left I was thinking to myself, "So that is what happened the other day. I'm lucky to be alive after all that."

A few days had passed and my family and girlfriend Mandy had been to visit. When I finally got released from hospital I went back to the scene where I got struck by lightning and I saw the tree I was running under and saw the shape of the lightning bolt carved into the bark of the tree.

I thought, "That looks like a Firestick."

Sea Green

Ellen Cregan

"SO RYDER, TELL me about this girl."

"Dad."

"What? Come on, you have been going out with her for a month now and you haven't even told me her name."

"I'm hanging up now. Bye Dad."

I know I should tell him about her. I don't know why I don't tell him. It's just I've never felt this way about a girl before. I know that's really cheesy – even I can't believe I just said that – but it's true. Her name is Alethea and she is the most beautiful in the city. I'm not just saying that because I am going out with her. If you asked any guy in the city who the best-looking girl was they would say Alethea. I would put money on that. How do I describe her? She has big, sea green eyes. Long hair, blonde with red tints. She is always smiling, which is a good thing because she has a nice smile.

"Don't tell me you're thinking about that girl again."

That would be Chase. His name isn't really Chase, it's Tracy. As you could imagine he got teased about that a lot in high school so he changed it to Chase. We suggested he could be called Trace but he didn't like that. He said there was a girl at his old school whose nickname was Trace.

"Are you coming tonight?" Chase asked, not waiting for an answer on his first question.

"What is tonight?"

"Party at Leroy's. Everyone is going, even Alethea."

I have to admit here, it was the mention of Alethea that made my decision. "Yea, I'll be there. I'll see ya tonight. I have some stuff I need to take care of." I don't really have anything that I need to do right now; I just needed to get away from Chase. He's a nice guy, I just feel bad for him. You see, his last relationship ended badly for him. Before I met Alethea we were, in a way, brought closer together as friends because we were both single. So now whenever Alethea or any other girl is mentioned I feel bad. He says he is fine but I can tell he isn't. Actually I do have things I should be doing. For one, looking for a job. I got fired from my last job as an accountant and now I am jobless at twenty nine. Maybe I will go join a trade, become a brickie.

RING RING

It's Dad. I consider pushing the ignore button but decide I should pick up and hope he still isn't trying to get information off me about Alethea.

"Hello."

"Ryder, I have to speak to you. Can you come to the house later?"

"Can't you tell me now?"

"It's important."

"Okay, I'll swing by later. Bye."

I decide to drop by on my way to Leroy's party. Right now I need to find a job. I open the newspaper and start circling jobs I might be capable of doing. I spend an hour looking for jobs before deciding that I should get ready for the party. I get dressed and head out to meet Dad at the house.

The drive takes about 20 minutes and by the time I get there the sun is almost set. When I get out of my car something doesn't feel right. I look around me to see if anyone else is here. No one. Stepping onto the rock path up to the door I keep looking around just to check that there isn't anyone there. I am about 10 metres from the door when I notice the door is open a bit. Something is definitely not right here. Before entering the house I peer around the door, checking there isn't anyone there. When I am sure there isn't anyone there I step into the house. The house is a mess. There is smashed glass everywhere, most of the paintings on the wall have been ripped off and are now lying on the floor. As I walk further into the house the scenery gets worse. Couches and chairs have been ripped apart and draws have been pulled out of cupboards and emptied onto the floor. Some of the floorboards have been pulled up and there are even some holes in the wall. Someone was here looking for something. My mind switches from one thought to the next in a matter of seconds. Then the thought crosses my mind. Where are my parents? A wave of panic suddenly sweeps across me.

"Dad! Mum! Where are you?"

Silence.

I call again. "DAD! MUM! SAY SOMETHING!" In the next room I hear some coughing. It sounds like Dad.

"Ryder, in here!" He doesn't sound good so I don't waste any time getting to him. When I get into the kitchen I have to stop for a second. It doesn't just look like someone had been looking for something in here. It looks like there was a fight. I find Dad behind a table that has been tipped over. He looks like he has been in a fight. He has a cut lip and what looks like some bruising around his left eye and cheek. It also looks like blood on his shirt but I can't see any cuts on him so it can't be his blood.

"Dad, what happened here?"

Although there doesn't seem to be any major wounds on him, he sounds like there are more injuries that I can't see. "They came, they were looking for something."

"Who came? What were they looking for?"

"Vittorio. He came. He was looking for the stone."

"What stone?"

"I didn't want you to have to worry about this. I thought it had been forgotten about. I am only telling you now because I might not make it."

"Don't talk like that. You're fine."

"No, I'm not. There is a stone that has been passed down through this family. It possesses many powers. Powers you can't imagine. I need you to get it. In the bedroom there is a power switch in the right hand corner. It looks like a power switch but it's not. One pull and it should open. Inside it is the stone. I want you to take it and protect it. With your life. Promise me you will protect it."

"Okay, I will. I promise."

And just like that, he was gone.

The Sumptuous Sounds of Nature

Gordon Crossin

THE CHATTERING BIRDS made her smile, until she heard a growl. It definitely wasn't a dog's growl, something far deeper, an almost indistinguishable rumble.

Probably just the echoing rumble of thunder in the distance, she assumed.

Surely if it was an animal growling the birds wouldn't be gathering around her chattering and chirping.

Soon the delightful little chittering birds gave way to the warbling of magpies, the laughter of kookaburras and the faarking of ravens.

Candace marched on unperturbed through the dense bush. Being a strong-willed woman her ex-husband said that she was as hardheaded and single minded as the Tassie devils and thylocenes she studied.

For several days now she had been slogging hard through the thickest and most inhospitable forest of Northwest Tasmania.

It is a place of rugged beauty, uninhabited and untouched by humanity.

Following the spore of a very large animal she was intrigued by the creature's unusual path.

It seemed to double back on itself every five kilometres or so.

At first she thought it was one of the locals hunting in the area, but there was no evidence of a bootprint or even a partial footprint, only the odd rock pushed into the ground or a broken or bruised leaf.

The birds seemed to be gathered around her, which she found strange with this place being so far from human habitation.

Almost imperceptibly the thick brush thinned, giving way to open up into a natural amphitheatre, a large depression in the ground covered by a bright green blanket of knee-high ferns.

The cacophony of raucous warbles and faarks reached a deafening crescendo as she entered the pretty little opening.

Suddenly the cacophony stopped. Silence.

She could now hear the direction of the intermittent growling on the other side of the clearing just in front of her...or was it behind her...

Quickly she turned around to the sounds of snapping underbrush. Nothing there!

Just the eerie glare of birds all around her in the trees. Kookaburras, magpies and large jet-black ravens staring at her as if in shock like a hushed audience at the coliseum as the emperor presents his sideways pointing thumb.

A desperate breathless squawk echoed through the bush behind her.

A figure crashed stumbling through the trees, staggering and then dropping to his knees. The sounds of desperate ragged breathing flooded her senses.

She could feel her heart in her throat as she stood dumbstruck in the presence of the enormous, muscular, dark form materialising from the shadows.

The prostrate figure slowly stopped scampering backwards in her direction.

Both of them were transfixed and frozen in awesome horror as the hulking man-beast reared up to a full height over seven feet tall and roared a primordial howl so terrible Candace shook uncontrollably with warm fluid pouring down her legs.

The fiend pounced with lightning grace, extending out an unnaturally long arm that swatted the hip of its victim with a resounding smack, sending him cartwheeling through the air like a rag doll.

Claws slashed into the helpless figure, sending gouts of blood flying through the air, setting a crimson sunset against the sky.

Massive jaws ripped into the gargling throat with claws tearing the head off with a horrible sucking sound.

Then with mouth dripping gore, the beast stared at her with pure malevolent evil.

Her blood turned to ice and a horrific scream filled her ears. Her throat ran dry and ragged. She then realised that it was in fact her own inhuman scream.

She doubled over as something wet smacked into her chest. She looked down to see that she held in her arms the severed head. His dead eyes bored into her very soul. She saw a warped caricature of her own face within those dead eyes. She saw her mouth stretched open gaping impossibly and her own eyes rolled back in her head as if in seizure.

She then heard the horrid laughter, the fiendish laughter that comes not from a human throat but from something far, far older than mankind.

Suddenly the spell was broken and she ran. She ran like she had never run before.

Adrenaline propelled her ever forward for what seemed like kilometres.

Hours later she collapsed into an exhausted heap, unable to keep her legs moving, her lungs about to burst with her heart thumping in her ears.

But she could still hear that soul destroying noise that she knew was her inescapable fate...

The wet snapping sound of crunching bone and moist rending flesh!

If Only You Knew

Michael Henderson

I LOVE MY mum. Very much.

I watch her. I watch her because she is like me.

I feel like I should know her better. So I watch.

But, she confuses me.

She does weird things. Silly things. Things I would not do.

I wish I could hug her. I think it would help. A big hug, like a great big blanket.

She once hugged me like that. Before I had to go.

One day I will.

At night I watch her, while she sleeps. She starts her sleep peaceful. She tosses back and forth till she kicks her sheets off. Her legs do funny things. People tell me it is a cramp, but I don't know what that is. I see her curl up tight and grimace. I know she wakes after a cramp. She wakes and needs to stand up. I laugh at this, but I know I shouldn't.

She never laughs.

When she wakes likes this she always drives to the beach. The beach looks peaceful. Beautiful. That must be why she goes. She always drives to the same spot. There are never any other cars; there are never any other people. She gets out of her car and stands in the dark. Then she walks toward the water.

Sometimes she pauses at the only light, where the grass ends and the sand begins. If she pauses she always leans heavily on the handrail. She always stands in the cold water, up to her knees. The waves thud into her. That's all she does. Stands. She never swims. She never sits on the beach and watches the waves. She stands. For hours. Her fingers touch her belly. They touch her big smiley scar. She stands like this till the sun comes up.

I watch her face. And I try to understand what she is doing. But I don't.

Her face looks like a doll's face. Her normal face is different. But I don't know how.

I think she wants something. If I could, I would tell her that no other adults are there. I would tell her that only God is there and only he can answer her questions. Sometimes I think she wants help; sometimes I think she doesn't; sometimes I don't know.

One time she walked on.

I did not like this. I could tell it was not good.

Her face was like a doll, but also tired. Tears fell down her face. I enjoyed watching the tears became part of the ocean. The tears looked beautiful in the night, all silvery and glistening. I did not like watching my mum.

She walked very slow.

She did not stop.

She did not stop.

Waves hit her. The water became deep. But she kept walking.

When the water was around her neck a wave knocked her over. I yelled for her to get up. But she did not. She just lay there. Floating for a moment, before she started to go down.

She drifted with the swell.

I watched.

I cried.

I prayed.

When she went down, into the water, she had a smile on her face. People have tried to explain to me what this meant, but I don't understand.

I pleaded with God. I begged my God to stop it.

The waves got bigger. She slumped and floated to the surface. People tell me she was unconscious. I do not understand what that means. The waves sucked and pushed her back to the beach. She was washed up and on to the sand. She lay there for a long time. Still. She was not breathing. She did not move. The waves gently washed around her, mixing the sand with her hair. I wanted to comb it and make it neat.

Then she coughed. She also vomited. She started breathing. She didn't move. She lay there for a very long time.

The sun rose and made the sky a pretty pink and purple.

After a long time, she got up and drove home and had a shower.

My dad asked, "How is this possible?"

My mum said, "I don't know, exactly. Aren't you excited?" She thought a moment. "I know I am."

"I am too. It's just…"

"What?"

"It's huge. For us." He paused, his hand touching the bed frame. "I thought you couldn't have kids. When did that change?"

"When I found out I was pregnant. You knew there was always the possibility."

My dad nodded. "But, I thought you wanted to move to London this year."

"I do. We are. This doesn't change that."

"But this is what you wanted."

"Of course. I want both."

"But you're the one who always talked about wanting a baby."

"What are you saying?"

"Nothing. It's a shock."

"I wouldn't say it like that. It certainly isn't the surprise I was expecting." I saw her touch her empty wedding ring finger.

My mum wrote "brand new, never used" on a card and looked at it. She did not like it. She dropped it on the ground and wrote the same words on another card. She put big curls on the word "never" and said, "I bet Mia would have written like that."

That's my name. Mia. I like my name. But I can't write. And I like pretty colours more than curls.

My mum drew three small hearts under the words. She put the card in front of some small booties.

An old lady picked up the booties and asked, "How much?"

"Sorry," said my mum. She did not look up.

"How much are these booties?"

"What does the card say?"

"It doesn't have a price."

My mum raised her voice. "They're sixty dollars."

The old lady put the booties down. "Sixty dollars? They're booties. The television over there is only fifteen dollars."

My mum's friend came over. She said sorry to the old lady, then lifted the booties from the table and whispered to my mum, "Let's put these inside. We don't need to sell everything."

"This stuff needs to go. And sixty dollars is a fair price." My mum grabbed the booties and thumped them down on the table. "Someone will love them."

The old lady walked off with a screwed up cranky face. "Good luck selling those."

My mum sat and cried in the corner of her new apartment. The apartment was empty of furniture. She looked out a window at the clouds. I like clouds too.

Her door bell rang and it was loud. She did not move.

She looked at a picture on the floor. It was a picture of my unborn sister. It is called an ultrasound, so I am told. The picture lay on the floor next to her foot. Under her foot was a picture of my dad. Her foot was slowly tearing it in two.

My mum's friend opened the door and kind of fell inside and spilt the boxes she was carrying across the floor. Her face was angry. But when she saw my mum her face changed and she gave her a hug. "Let's get a coffee. There's a café around the corner."

At the café, my mum's friend asked, "Have you heard from the father?"

"No. And I'm pleased about it."

"He doesn't want to be involved?"

"I don't want him involved."

A little boy skidded under my mum's table and bumped into her. She rubbed her leg. The boy looked worried. My mum smiled her broad warm smile at the boy. The same smile she had given me when she held me that one time. She looked at the boy's mum and her smile broadened further. She guided the boy round the table and back to his mum.

The boy's mum said thank you.

My mum said, "He's cute. How old is he?"

The boy's mum smiled. "Two. Is this your first?" she asked, pointing at my mum's tummy.

"No, it's my second."

The boy's mum looked around the café. "How old is your other one?"

"Mia would have been two."

The boy's mum looked puzzled. Then she mumbled, "I'm sorry," and went back to her chair.

My mum's friend said, "I can't take you anywhere."

My mum smiled.

"How do you do it?"

"Do what?"

"Cope with other kids?"

"I don't know. Some days I love it – some days I hate it. Isn't that normal? What do you do?"

"If he had rammed into my leg I would have told him off."

"He was only playing. Like what Mia would have done."

"Mia."

"She would have been a beautiful little girl. She would have played like that."

My mum's friend looked stunned. "How will you cope when number two is here?"

"Cry. Then smile. Then do both again and again till I forget to do one, or the other."

"And God?"

"He's still there. I just wish he'd take away the heartache."

The car made a loud noise as it stopped at the entrance to the hospital.

My dad said calmly, "Come on."

My mum yelled, "I've lost her. I've lost her. I know it."

"You don't know that."

"I can feel it."

My mum got out of the car. My dad saw the car seat and his face changed. My mum turned around and saw the blood and started to cry.

My dad said, "Leave it. It's just a little blood. We can clean it later. It doesn't mean you've lost her." And he led her inside the hospital.

A doctor came out and took them to an ultrasound room. He started poking my mum's belly.

My mum begged, "Is she okay?"

The doctor didn't reply. He just kept poking and feeling.

The doctor grunted and my mum asked, "What? What is it?"

The doctor just smiled and said, "I'll know more in a minute. Just relax."

That day was like now. I knew everything was all right. But my mum didn't. And I could not tell her.

The doctor pushed a little too hard, and I pushed back. This made the doctor smile.

Through the doctor's machine my mum and dad heard my heart beat. The doctor said I was fine.

My mum relaxed.

My dad relaxed.

I relaxed.

We all relaxed till four months later, when we rushed to the hospital again.

All our lives are eternal.

They appear trapped by time and space. They seem stuck to earth. But it is not so. They go on. The eternal has no past or present or future. It just is.

I just am.

I get to watch my mum. I can see one day at a time.

One day we will all know this.

Like I know.

Trust me – life is eternal.

One day we will all know that life on earth is like a party – full of promise, fun while it lasts, but over all too quick.

And then the rest of our lives will start.

One day my mum will know this too.

One day I will get to look into her eyes, and she will look into mine. She will see my eyes as they really are. Not how she imagines them to be. I will wrap my arms around her. She will wrap her arms around me. And we will both know that everything is all right.

One day I will.

Haiku

Mary Arch

Seashell's cochlear
sanctum, holy of holies
Christ, my hiding place

Outstretched eucalypt
scarlet blood sap dripping down
echoes Golgotha

Passport to Nowhere

Bruce Lyman

D AMN. SHE DIDN'T know passports even had an expiry
date. What good was a boyfriend if he didn't tell you
these sorts of details? She banged the counter in frustration.

"But this is MY passport. Can't you see the photo? It really is
me."

The border control guard, squashed into his tiny booth,
didn't blink. The sweat poured down his neck in a grimy collar
two sizes too small, and clearly not washed in the last month.
Tattered military ribbons hung lopsided over his breast pocket.

"I do not care for your passport miss." His somnolent bass
rumbled over her and told her he could care less. He rumbled
some more.

"And I do not care for your shout miss." He locked sleepy
eyes at her and lifted an eyebrow, waiting for her response.

She looked across the aisle to see Rory pass through the
checkpoint. He smiled and waved at her, signaled he was off to
the bathroom, turned and was gone. She looked back at the
guard.

"Your passport is run out of time miss. You need to see the
supervisor." He raised a giant hand and a small, immaculately
dressed man appeared at the back of the booth.

"Her passport has run out of time. You need to fix it for her."

The older man had a friendly smile. He waved her to a small office with no window.

"Do not worry miss. Every problem can be fixed." He closed the door and sat down, leaving her standing.

He hunched over the document, thumbing through it, tut-tutting and sucking in his breath as if he was reading something disastrous. After thumbing through it a number of times, pausing now and then to examine this or that visa, he opened the top left-hand draw and consulted an old green manual. Finally he pulled the phone across the desk and spun the dial. The conversation did not sound encouraging. She heard him mutter, "But she can't stay here," and "The visa is expired too."

"That's odd," she thought. "I must have been travelling far too long. I don't think I even had a visa for this place." She fought down a moment of panic. This could be worse than she thought.

Finally he hung up the phone and exhaled a long and weary breath.

"That will be one hundred US dollars please. Cash."

"What?"

"Your exit stamp has been approved. But the administration fee is one hundred US dollars. Cash only."

With the passport stamped she finally caught up with Rory who was roaming the single, small duty free shop that had more bare shelves than full.

"Phew that was close. I thought I was never going to get out of this dump."

"How do you mean?" Rory was puzzled.

"Turns out my passport had expired while we were here."

Rory screwed up his face. "That doesn't sound right. When was it supposed to expire?"

"Uh, I don't know. Let me have a look."

She extracted her passport and opened it to the photo page and checked the date. Her heart sank.

"And?" Rory quizzed.

She put the passport back in her backpack and blushed.

"You don't need to know."

Rory grinned.

Mandy Meets Billy

Stephen Chan

I'M NOT THE main attraction at this small zoo. The tigers are, of course. But I'm not jealous of *them*. They are the princes of the animal kingdom, after all. I'm just one of the paupers. No – it's the other animals I'm thinking about. The ones inside this enclosure with me. The sort you can pet and feed and pose with for a photo. Why *they* always get more attention than me is the thing that really gets my horns hot.

Everyone likes Barney and Belinda. Because they can hop, I suppose. Big deal – even I could hop if it wasn't for my arthritis. And Belinda wears that bumbag with young Jojo in it. How *cute*, you all say. Cute my hoof! Spoilt little brat, is what I think. Why can't he walk around by himself like I had to at his age? Then there's Felicia and Giselle. You all like *them*, because they're graceful and gentle-eyed. As for me, well – I'm just a goat.

If I sound bitter and cynical, I have good reason. It seems that everyone except me has something they can use to win friends. Charm, talent, prestige, intelligence – all part of that illusory thing called charisma. But was there ever a creature so devoid of charisma as a goat? Never mind the millions of mouths we feed with our milk. All you people want is charisma! Well, I don't have it, so just leave me alone or boil me in a stew for all I care!

Every now and then though, something happens that makes me wish things were different, that makes me hope perhaps we could be friends. Those rare occasions when I get a little bit of attention. Hang on – there could be one coming right now in fact.

Hello there, child. You talking to me? A photo? Why, certainly – well, I'm flattered. Come to think of it, I really am a rather handsome chap, as I've been told countless times by my mother and ... others I can't remember right now. Just stand next to me, smile for the camera, and ... goat's cheese!

Now what's that in your hand? You want to feed me? Why, of course – how very kind of you. What've you got there? The seed and nut combo? Mmm ... not bad. I do prefer the fruit and berry mix, though. By the way, please do *not* call me Billy. My name is Oscar – Oscar, okay?

Hey, what are you doing now? Stroking my beard? Oh, thank you, quite a fine beard, I know. Okay, child – that's enough for now. It's making me feel a little nervous. Did you hear that? I said *stop*. Listen, I'm serious – that's enough! I am *not* your pet! I do have dignity you know! There is nobility in my blood. I am descended from the great mountain goats of Switzerland! I am warning you – one more touch and ... right! That's it! I have no other option but to ... *charge*!

Oh dear! What have I done? No, child – please don't cry. I'm awfully sorry. I know, I know. I'm just a rotten little so-and-so. Okay, you go and tell your Daddy how bad I am.

Bother! I think I've just lost another friend. And she was *so* nice!

He is an Old Cat

Bruce Lyman

He is an old cat
Shrinking every day
Into his baggy black
Suit of knobbly bone and
Matted fur.

He is a not so young cat
As he once was flopping
Into favourite spots: now
Instead a careful, cautious
Setting into place.

He is the same old cat
With which we are
Comfortable ruling our
Place; yellow eyed glare at
Our unruliness.

He is an ageless cat
Folded into strange parts
In the fallen leaves of autumn

Grooming and licking the matt
Into lace.

He is a cool old cat
Baleful stare ignoring
The titch titch incitement
To misbehave; far too mature
For that.

Today, a very young cat;
Smooth, wetted down lace
Drying in the sun. Yellow eyed
Stare, unblinking from his
Sunny nest.

Casualties

Dylan Dunkley

I T WAS A sight no-one wanted to see. Lying on the ground in front of me was fourteen year-old Jessica Keller. She had been missing for six days and her mum was worried sick. It was my unfortunate job to tell Mrs Keller her daughter had been murdered. After seven years doing this job, I still hadn't gotten used to it. I turned and started walking towards my old 1989 Subaru Brumby. I got it when I was fifteen and a half years old. She was my first car and, now, my only car.

My train of thought was interrupted by the all too familiar voice of my partner, Alex Boziko. Everyone just called him Booze, which was a nickname I gave him in year five. Booze and I had been friends since year two, and we trust each other with our lives. By the end of high school I wanted to be a doctor and Booze wanted to be an author. Instead we both ended up working for the Taree Police Department, and now we got promoted from cop to detective. Well, it was seven years ago but it still feels like yesterday.

"What we got?" Booze asked me as he climbed out of his fancy Aston Martin DB9.

Unlike me, Booze had no problem with his cash flow.

"A dead fourteen year-old girl."

"How long has she been ... occupied?"

"The M.E. says ninety six hours."

"Do they have any idea how?"

"She was tortured, then after that she was drugged."

"So which one did she die of?"

"Definitely the drugs. Well, at least that's what the M.E. thinks."

"How was she tortured?"

"Her fingernails were pulled out along with her teeth. Plus there were numerous cuts to her chest and arms. Her eyes were found in an esky filled with ice twenty feet away from the victim. They were expertly removed."

"Ouch."

"No. The M.E. says that the sicko removed the eyes after she was dead."

By this time I was in my car.

"You know those cars are like really ancient history. They're like, twenty years old," Booze said as he leaned into the window like he always does.

"I know, but I love her and wouldn't give her up for anything."

"Where you going?"

"I have to tell the mother."

"Good luck then."

"Thanks. I'll need it."

As I drove towards Mrs Keller's house, questions started to flood into my head. Why Jessica? What had she done? What kind of psycho monster would do such a thing? What was he looking for?

As I reached for the doorbell, I thought about how much pain this would cause Mrs Keller. Her husband had died from a heart attack three weeks before and her son Bill Keller had committed suicide just one week ago.

I pushed the doorbell. No-one answered, so I rang it again. Still nothing.

"Mrs Keller? Hello? Are you home?"

I pulled my gun from my thigh holster. I kicked open the door and started scanning the room. My eyes immediately glued to the one thing that stood out in that room. The horrible, gruesome, disgusting sight lying on the ground in front of me.

I couldn't move, because lying in front of me was Amanda Keller. A knife had been plunged into her right eye and she had two gunshot wounds, one in the chest, the other in her leg. Her fingernails had been pulled out just like Jessica's except this time the killer put them into a plastic container.

There was no way in the world she was alive but I checked her pulse anyway. I heard a car pull up outside. I lifted my gun to chest height then jumped beside the door. The door opened with a creaking noise that echoed through the house. As soon as I saw the tiniest part of the person, I spun around and lifted my gun to the man's head.

"What are you doing here?" I asked.

"Chill Dyl, it's me, Booze."

I breathed in slowly and put the gun back into its holster.

"What's been taking you so long?" Booze said as his eyes started to scan the room. He stopped at the dead figure lying on the ground. "Oh, right. Do you think it could've been the same killer?"

"Yeah, most of the things the killer did to Jessica he did to Amanda."

"Have you called Arty?"

"No, not yet."

Booze pulled out his fancy Samsung mobile phone and pushed a few buttons. He then put the phone to his ear and walked outside.

About twenty minutes later the M.E. turned up. He was about fifty-two. His son and wife both died in a car crash two years ago. His name was Arthur Fredo but we just called him Arty for short.

Arty climbed out of his van and started walking towards us.

"Another one?"

"Yeah, unfortunately."

We heard a crash come from behind the van.

A head popped out from behind the van and said, "Sorry sir, I tripped."

"It's okay Tim," Arty replied.

"Who's that?" I asked Arty.

"That's my new assistant. His name is Timothy Ruddingworth. He's twenty two and fresh out of university."

"How long has he been working with you?"

"Two weeks, and good except a little clumsy."

There was another crash from behind the van and out limped pale looking Tim. He was carrying a large tool box that looked quite heavy.

"Where do want the tool box, sir?"

"Over by the body, and stop calling me sir."

Tim carried the heavy tools over to the dead body, then stood staring at the dead body. The look on his face said that he had seen it before.

"Is there something wrong?" Arty asked.

"No, nothing wrong, just looking. You've got to admire the use of imagination and skill that the killer used."

"What skill and imagination. There's no skill or imagination in killing someone. Now stop admiring and giving the killer credit and find out who the hell did this."

It looked as if Tim wasn't even listening to me. I walked towards my car and opened the door. I climbed in and as I was closing the door, there were creaks and cracks. I put the old rusty key into the ignition and started her up.

Booze leaned into the window.

"Where you going partner?" he asked.

"I've got some research to do."

"Call me if you find anything."

"I will."

The 'ding' of the elevator rang through the empty lab.

"Got anything yet Ussa?" I called out.

I watched as a head appeared out the side of one of the computers.

"Ahh, Dyl. As a matter of fact I do. Guess what I found on the fingernails."

I said nothing. Staring, waiting for the answer.

"Not in a guessing mood I see. Well, it looks like Jessica didn't go down without a fight. I found fragments of skin underneath her fingernails."

"But I thought her fingernails were removed."

"They were, but the skin had dried to the fingernail."

Ussa looked excited. As if she had something to say.

"What else you got?"

"I knew you'd ask. I was looking at the deaths of the other family members, and I discovered that Bill Keller didn't actually commit suicide."

She passed me a picture of the crime scene.

"See, the bed is tipped onto its end and the rope tied to the top end, and (as usual) the boy's head in the loop, right?"

"Yeah, I guess."

"Wrong, the rope is too short for a person his height to be able to commit suicide, and before you ask, the forensic pictures show that there was no chair in the room and the forensic reports say nothing about a trace of a chair. I asked Arty to check out the death of Henry Keller as well."

"Got anything back yet?"

"Nope."

"Keep me updated," I said as I headed back towards the elevator.

I pushed level two and as the doors were closing I heard Ussa say, "Good luck!"

The doors re-opened into a long room with rows of cold, hard, steel tables. I noticed Arty sitting at his desk looking through papers. I walked up behind him, leaned over and spoke into his ear.

"What ya got Arty?"

He immediately spun around.

"Oh, it's just you. I thought it was Tim. He's been acting a little strange ever since we found Jessica - he keeps on disappearing. Anyway, I'm guessing you're down here for the report on Henry Keller's death or should I say murder!"

"Murder? It was said it was a heart attack."

"It actually says in the report that Henry Keller actually did die of poison but I guess they must have said it was a heart attack for the public."

I felt my phone start to vibrate in my pocket. I pulled it out and pushed the answer button.

"Dunkley," I said into the brick-like Nokia.

"It's me – Booze – you've got to check this out!"

"I'll be there in a minute."

When the doors to the elevator opened Booze was standing right in front of it.

"Follow me," he said.

He led me to his desk which was covered in folders and reports. On the left of his desk was a picture of his wife. His wife had red hair with dark brown eyes. On the right were his two kids, John and Julie. John had short black hair like his dad and dark brown eyes like his mum. Julie had blonde hair and blue eyes. The blue eyes were from her dad and they made her look sweet and innocent. The background of his computer was a picture of him and his wife on their honeymoon in Hawaii. Booze pushed a few buttons on the keyboard of his computer and a picture of a man in an army uniform popped up.

"His name is Phil Keller. He is Harry Keller's brother. Family friends of the Kellers say that Phil and Harry have been having a little fight that has been going on for ages. Not just verbal, physical too."

"Do we know where he is?"

"Well, according to his commander he went on leave for a month. I know a bit long but I think he may have bribed someone, and before you ask he is staying at The Botley Inn, fifty six Manning Road, cabin twenty seven."

We both decided to go in Booze's car just because it looked better. We arrived at the inn at a little past two p.m..

"Which way is cabin twenty-seven?" I asked the young looking boy at the front desk.

He pointed towards the left exit. "That way but I'm afraid I'm not allowed to let you go through under privacy rules."

I held up my badge. "How about now?"

We started looking at the cabin numbers go past. Twenty-three, twenty-four, twenty-five, twenty-six and finally twenty-seven. I knocked on the tall, white, wooden door. There was no answer so I tried once more. Still nothing.

I pulled my gun from its holster and reached for the door handle. I pushed down and surprisingly the door was open. I heaved the door the rest of the way and lifted my gun to chest height. I started scanning the room. I was expecting to find a dead body on the floor, but there wasn't any. I signalled for Booze to check out the right side of the house while I checked the left. Six minutes later (six minutes is a long time to check a room) I had finished checking the first of the two rooms. When I walked into the second I froze. I saw two objects that were laid out perfectly on the bed as if someone wanted someone else to find them. The first one was a gun in a clear plastic bag. The second was a bloody knife.

I heard the front door open, then footsteps. The footsteps were coming towards where I was. I hid beside the doorway and waited. When I saw the tiniest bit of the man, I jumped on him. I took him to the ground and held my gun to his head.

"Who are you?" I said to him.

"I'm Phil Keller, who the hell are you?"

By this time Booze was already in the room. He saw the knife and gun. I pulled out my handcuffs and handcuffed Phil's hands.

"Read him his rights," I said to Booze.

Later Booze, Ussa and I were standing around Booze's desk, celebrating our victory. We had caught the criminal. His fingerprints were on the gun and the blood on the knife was confirmed as Jessica's and Amanda's. Something wasn't sitting right with me.

"Where's Arty?" I asked Ussa.

"He said he had some work to do."

I started going through the case files. Something wasn't right. It was all too obvious. I walked over to my desk and searched some things on the computer. I clicked on a few things and a screen popped up. I sat staring, hoping I wasn't reading what I thought I was. I got up and started running towards the elevator.

"What's wrong Dyl?" Booze called out after me but I wasn't listening.

I started frantically pushing the up-down button. It was taking too long. I ran towards the stairs and I started running down them. I stopped at the door I was looking for. I lightly pushed open the door and I saw Arty sitting at his very confined workspace, reading. I was about to walk in when I saw a glint of metal. I stared at the glint of metal and noticed it was moving. I pulled my gun from its holster and pushed open the door.

"Freeze!" I yelled.

Arty turned around. "What's going on?" he asked.

I saw the glint of metal was a knife and the person holding the knife was Timothy Ruddingworth.

"I knew it," I shouted. "Drop it!"

I walked up behind Tim and pulled his hands behind his back.

"You really thought you were going to get away with it?" I asked. "Arty, you are not looking at Tim Ruddingworth, you are looking at Robert Ludsmen." I started explaining as I pulled the knife out of Robert's hand.

I chucked the knife to the ground and it made a loud clang.

"Robert used to work with Henry Keller in the army but got a dishonourable discharge for trying to shoot Henry. It was noted that before Robert got shipped out he made a threat to Henry that one day he would repay the favour. Later Robert got arrested for multiple counts of murder using the same techniques he used on our two victims, Jessica and Amanda. He escaped from prison two months ago but the cops gave up after a month."

I felt steel slide into my left leg and I looked down to see a small pocketknife in Robert's hand. I felt the pain immediately but I tried to ignore it. I pulled my gun out of its holster once again and raised it above my head.

"My turn," I said and I thumped him over the head with the butt of my gun.

The pain started to kick in and I collapsed. But Booze appeared just in time to catch me.

"I heard the whole thing Dyl. Nice work," Booze said.

"Case closed!" I replied.

"That's right partner, case closed."

Riley

Bruce Lyman

RILEY'S TRAINING FOR Vietnam came at the expense of the goats that lived in the scrub behind the old house. The rifle seemed to bang away all morning, sometimes crackingly close, other times softly distant, a faint and inoffensive pop. Every now and then Riley would appear near the house, stripped to his shorts, goat carcass draped over his shoulders. Did we ever eat these? I don't recall. In my seven year old mind I think they were only there to impress. And it was impressive, no question about it. Riley's chest was slick with blood and his shorts were laced with it. The carcasses would be dropped and Riley would silently return up the hill and the cracking and popping would soon resume. I fancy the goats were simply used as "dog tucker".

When we first purchased the property the place was overrun with manuka and gorse. It took a while to chop our way in and to carve out the original farm house, well and shed from the closed ranks of feral weeds and timber. I close my eyes and open my mind forty years later and smell the goat manure in the shed, the mustiness of it mingling with the smell of possum droppings. Old horse leather was still there and an old rusty tractor of some sort, its damp diesel and oil long soaked into the earth. Even to a youthful mind there was a sense of opening a sacred place, a sanctuary of memories and other people's dreams. All failed. The drifting dust in the laser beams of light that radiated from nail holes in the roofing iron dared us to disturb those memories. They made us think twice about treading there.

It was the days of Vietnam. 1968. Images of conflict on the neighbour's television set when the cartoons were overtaken by the news. On the old black and white box in the front bedroom of Mrs Paton's. When we visited there on a Sunday afternoon we might, if it was raining only mind you, watch a Western. The goodies would defeat the baddies in a hail of last stand bullets, all would be set to rights with the railroad and the ranchers and before we knew it the black and white magic box had transported us from Montana to Vietnam. It was an exotic and strange place but we knew there was a war happening there. The young men in the youth group would talk about the place. About the war. About fighting in the jungle and how they thought they would be good at it. Riley disappeared, and the cracking and popping ceased. The young men spoke about Riley going to Vietnam.

I don't think I saw another goat on the property. Pigs yes. Rabbits aplenty. Then Riley reappeared. More sober. More still. More silent. His shirt was stripped off and the cracking and popping recommenced. More itinerant. More distant. Then it stopped altogether and I never saw him on the property again. If I took a slight detour to school I could walk past his mother's house. It sat down off the road a little, retreated. Schoolboys talk. "Riley went back to Vietnam." "Riley went mad and went back to Vietnam." "He went mad being back here and had to go back to Vietnam." "Riley murdered someone and had to go back to

Vietnam." "Riley is a wild man and never went back to Vietnam. He is in the high country chasing deer." We would look at the lace curtains hiding the house secrets, turn and plod on. I left Riley in my mind's eye chasing goats with a lethal purposefulness. Forty years on he is still there. The goats are long gone.

The Goat Diaries

Mary Arch

MY NAME IS Whippersnipper. At least that's what they call me. My real name is Greg but these people are not to know. I have been assigned to their backyard. It's wild and I have my work cut out for me. There are a plenty of dandelions and shoulder high grass here but I'm sick of them already. I need a bit more gastronomic excitement.

What does interest me are those gerberas over the fence in the neighbour's yard. Now they're my favourite. I have just figured out a way to get to them. My owners both disappear for many hours each day so it shouldn't be a problem to carry out my plan without them noticing.

The problem is that there is a dog in the neighbour's yard. A beagle. He's a ridiculous thing. They call him Patches but his real name is Lesley. Goats haven't been known to outsmart dogs in the past but I'm about to change history.

Leather Chair

Bruce Lyman

This story was inspired by two random postcards placed together – one depicting a young man sitting in a chair, the other promoting an art show. The latter depicted a glass slipper covered in red glass beads. I started to write about the young man. The chair took over.

YOU MAY NOT think a leather chair is any big deal, or wonder how it came to be covered in blood. But where I come from the only leather I ever saw was breathing, and on four legs. And the blood was on the inside. So when I found the chair on the side of the road, upended with its four wooden legs pointed at the sky I stopped and looked around. The dense wall of plantation pine trees were silent observers and no one had rattled the road gravel for some time. Yet here it was, discarded and out of place. I looked around. Not a sound.

The shiny leather and deep seated brass button pinning down the crosshatch pattern across the seat and back distracted as I levered the heavy beast back onto its feet. At first I did not see the darkened stains leaking down its back or the pooling darkness on the seat. It was a beautiful chair and begging for me to sink into it. I looked around. The road was still empty and the forest silent, yet I felt as guilty as if I had entered the study of an important person and was intruding.

After some hesitation I eased into the seat. How comfortable was that? I was amazed at how hard it looked but how comfortable it proved to be. My feet stretched out into the long grass and nodding wildflowers and I leaned back to gaze into the sky. The day slowed down and I soaked up the sun. The chair was very comfortable. More comfortable than anything I had ever felt in my whole life. The back and seat sank back and the arm rests seemed to wrap me in and hold me firm. I felt I was floating on air. My eyes felt heavy and sluggish. "What the heck, just a small nap," I thought.

"Taking it easy as always, you layabout."

The laughter broke me out of my slumber and I struggled to get out of the chair in response to Ian's rasping laugh. He was always catching me out at the mill where we worked. There was no malice but still, he was always interrupting my short naps I like to take behind the timber stacks. The chair seemed to protest, springs squeaking and twanging and the leather creaking. Those arm rests were closer than I thought but I used them to lever myself away.

But even with their help I found my jeans and shirt were stuck to the leather by something sticky and adhesive, and leaving the comfort of the chair was more than just a battle to overcome my drowsiness. As I gained my feet Ian's chuckle stopped as he caught the sight of my back.

"Whoa, check that out. Looks like blood. What the heck have you found?"

That leather chair had blood on it. Only hours old. Ian stuck his fingers in the blackness and held them to the sun.

"Animal or human? Hard to tell," Ian mused to himself. I was struggling out of my T-shirt and paid him no attention. Suddenly I could hear the flies.

"Where did you find it?"

"Nowhere. Well, just here. It was lying upside down, looking like it had fallen off a truck."

"Thrown off more like it. You sure you found it?"

"What do you mean?"

"You haven't been splashing any blood around? Hey, you aren't hurt are you?"

"No, no, I don't think so."

Ian turned me around a few times and asked me to breathe in and out. Laughing, he asked me to touch my toes. I didn't think it was funny.

"What if it is human? What do I do now? If that is human, well, you know, you know…"

"That someone is dead?"

"Yeah, that's a lot of blood."

We both looked around the forest clearing. There were no other clues that told us anything about the bloody chair and how it got there.

"Come on, pick up your T-shirt and let's get back to town. That new copper is going to want to look at this. Maybe even those CSI types will come and poke around. That chair could have come from interstate."

"But the blood is too fresh."

Ian was already striding off and he yelled back at me. "Now you are thinking too hard about it. C'mon detective, there are experts who can worry about that sort of thing. All you have to worry about is getting those clothes cleaned."

The walk back to town took us about twenty minutes. Neither of us spoke. Ian did not seem too worried about what we had found but my head swirled with possibilities. Where had it come from? Whose blood was it? Will the coppers think we had killed someone and thrown the body away?

That is exactly what the young country policeman thought. He wanted to lock us up for our troubles until he could get advice from his headquarters. That was until Mrs Harrison walked into the station with a puzzled look on her face and handed a brown paper parcel over the counter. "You need to look at this young Constable. I think you might have the first murder of your career on your hands."

Ha, that got his attention. He carefully peered into the bag and then ripped it open until we could all see a glittering glass shoe lying beached on the Formica. It had a high heel and was decorated with ruby red glass crystals that flashed in the light.

We all gazed in silence at this shoe. I had never seen anything like it. Not even in the fancy magazine Howard sometimes stacked on the window sill at his barber shop. I was looking at the beads and wondering where a person would wear such a thing, and missed what Mrs Harrison was on about. It was soon the talk of the town even though the copper tried to keep it under wraps. You can't keep something like this from being spoken about in a country town. A foot was still in that fancy slipper, bone and flesh chopped off above the ankle.

It turns out the blood on the chair belonged to a dog. So the experts said. That creeped me out. Lots of blood but no hair, wondered the young copper. He thought that was strange. Because there was no human blood he stopped by the timber yard in his patrol car. The boss thought there was trouble and raised his hand to have the ripping saw stopped. As it whirred down the copper and the boss got into a huddle and kept looking over at me. I was trying to look busy but I don't think I fooled anyone. The boss waved me over.

"Simon here says he has some lost property of yours. Says you handed it in a couple of days ago."

"Lost property? Nah, I don't think so," I replied. I was a bit uneasy with Simon the copper talking to the boss. Might talk about the timber I was selling on the side. That would be unholy.

Simon wiped his forehead. "The chair you found. Dog blood. Can't say how it got there but I don't need that fancy furniture cluttering up my cells. Come and pick it up. It's all yours."

Ian, of course, laughed his head off. Silly mongrel. "Shoulda seen the look on your face when you realised you were not in trouble," he cackled. "Wish I had a camera. Or a video – would send it in to one of those TV video shows where…"

"Yeah, yeah, I know, very funny. But what am I going to do with that thing? There is no way I'm going to fit that chair into my room. The landlady will have a spasm and not cook breakfast for a week if I tried that on." But Ian, as always, had a sensible plan.

"Hey, we all know you like a quick cat nap behind the timber stacks every now and then. How about I bring my truck down to the station, pick up the chair and bring it back to work. It will be out of the weather and we can all enjoy it."

I could hardly argue with that so at the end of our shift we drove out through the plantations of pine into town and lifted the chair onto the truck.

"Phew, this thing must have a cast iron frame," grumbled Ian as he staggered under its weight, trying to gain the refuge of the tailgate. "There is more than just timber in the frame of this thing."

I had to agree. "It sure is heavy. But you know I was surprised by how comfortable it is, even though it is so bulky and looks hard as the boss's face. Try it when we get back to the yard. You'll be surprised."

"I'll do just that," Ian grunted from the other side of the chair. "It has been a hard day – a quick nap in the chair will do me a world of good."

We shunted the chair in behind the timber stacks where we took our lunch out of the sight of the boss. Then we both stood there and admired it.

Ian had a puzzled look on his face. "Strange thing you know mate. That blood looks just as fresh as it did all those days ago when you found it. When was that? Last Wednesday? Yeah, Wednesday. Strange. Here, I will clean it off and test it out like you said."

"Sure, go right ahead. I am off home for dinner. Don't appear for grace and that landlady of mine throws my dinner over the back porch railing. Worse than living at home."

Ian laughed and laughed. "Sure thing. Catch you tomorrow."

The boss was in a grumpy mood all the following day. Ian was his foreman and there was a big job on. But Ian was not at work. I told the boss I had seen Ian up here last night.

"Tell me something I don't know," he growled at me. "His truck is still here."

That surprised me. I wandered out to the parking lot to see for myself. Sure enough, there was Ian's battered old jalopy of a truck.

I wandered back to the timber stack and stepped behind it. The chair was there, still and shiny. I scratched my head, puzzled. Ian had said he would clean off the blood but clearly he had not. It was still as shiny and fresh as ever. That was just too weird and the skin goosebumped up my arms.

But there were no signs of Ian. No boots, lunch box, dropped keys. Nothing.

Ian was missing three days when his boots appeared beside the chair. I was the one who saw them first, just lying there as if they had been kicked off by someone sitting back in that chair. Now I really freaked out. That was too weird. I ran back to get the boss and asked him to call the copper. The boss stood and looked at the chair, and the boots, scratching his stubbly cheek. He frowned. "Bugger had better not be playing games with me, what with this big job on and all."

"Ian never played games with work stuff. Please call the copper. This ain't right."

The boss nodded and strode off to make the call.

Simon stood with his thumbs hitched in his belt, gazing at the chair and the boots at their feet.

"You sure they were not there three days ago?" he asked me.

"Yes sir."

"You playing games perhaps. Did you hide his boots and then place them out here?"

"No, of course not. Why would I do something like that?"

"Keep ya pants on, just asking the obvious questions before we have to think about the not so obvious."

After a short, silent pause the young copper stepped towards the chair and picked up one of Ian's well scuffed, unpolished boots. He looked puzzled as he straightened up and jigged his hand, as if feeling the weight of the boot. He turned the boot right way up and looked inside. He scared the bejeesus out of all of us when he shouted and dropped the boot. Even the boss turned pale and took a step back. The cop picked the boot up again, more gingerly this time, and tilted it to show us the contents. Bone and flesh.

This town of four hundred lumber people has not had so much excitement since a drunk deer shooter shot holes in Mr Macintosh's fuel bowser and that was twelve years ago. Mr Mac never repaired those holes and tells the story like it was a rerun of D-Day. The copper got all the excitement he needed with a white van up from the headquarters with FORENSICS stencilled along the side and a refrigeration unit built into it. That got the old-timers talking. Everyone reckoned a killer was on the loose.

I had found Ian's boots so I was called in to the police station to answer a powerful lot of questions. On and on they went. I could tell them nothing but I think they were suspicious of me. Soon they were done.

"You are not planning on going anywhere now are you?"

"Yeah, sure. Going back to work. The boss has lost Ian and I am down here talking to you. Someone needs to give him a hand."

The big shot forensic copper did not react. "Stay in town," was all he said.

I was about to leave when Mrs Harrison was brought in. She smiled at me and I think for a moment we were in a small but special group together. The "bone in boot finders" group, an elite club in this town. I nearly laughed at the thought of it but the police were straight into Mrs Harrison, no pleasantries if you please. I kept my mouth shut.

"Where did you find that glass slipper? Tell us straight."

"Well, as I already told your young colleague here – he wrote it all down you know – and I signed that it was all correct, ahh... Well, as I said, I was walking my dog along Cable Lane. He loved the woods that dog. But he has been gone a week you know and I cannot find him. I can't for the life of me think where he might be."

"The slipper?"

"Ah yes. Well actually it was not a slipper we found first. It was a leather chair. Bovver barked and jumped all over it. He was very excited by it. Jumped straight up on the seat whining and barking and sniffing at it. Then he just curled up on it and looked like he was going to have an afternoon snooze. Silly dog. I wonder where he is. Have you boys seen a black Labrador anywhere in your travels by any chance?"

"Mrs Harrison, tell us about the slipper."

"I am getting there, young man. Just be patient. If I hurry through then you will only want to be asking me more questions later. A stitch in time you know."

I thought the policemen from the city looked irritated but they only nodded and Mrs Harrison continued her story.

"Well, here's the thing – I could hardly get Bovver off the chair. My husband named him you know. Bovver is not something I would offend an animal with. He did not want to leave and scratched the leather a little I am sorry to say. It was when I was trying to drag that blessed animal off the chair when I noticed the shoe in the grass. 'What a weird place to leave such a pretty shoe,' I thought. But there was not much time for pleasant thoughts 'coz I saw the contents straight away you know. It gave me such a start. But I have seen worse you know, I was a nurse during the war. Sat in hospital ships off the coast of New Guinea. Saw some messy stuff. So this chopped off foot was no big deal. But our plantations are not a war zone and I wanted to get it reported to young Simon straight away. Trouble was, he was out of town talking to farmers in Hillsdale about cattle thieving so I hear. So I had to come in and report it the next day. Kept the shoe in the meat cooler you know. Don't want flies ruining things for you all. His first murder you know, young Simon. This will look good on his report. Darn that Bovver. I forgot all about him until after I got home. He must have got lost in the plantation. He will come home sometime I hope. All you policemen sure you haven't seen a lost Labrador? He will answer to 'Bovver' if you speak to him nicely. Even you boys from the city."

The "young Simon" as she called him suddenly noticed I was still standing at the counter. "You can leave now thanks. We will call you if we need to ask any more questions." He was sounding all official like, trying to impress the heavies from FORENSICs. I said nothing and made my way back to the timber yard. I felt sad for Mrs Harrison and her Bovver, though the name made me laugh. Back at work the boss was too busy writing up advertisements for a new foreman. He was not cutting timber that day. "Too much on my mind," he said. "Why don't you go and sort some of that paneling we cut for the school contract? Don't rush, no point right now."

But I needed to do something to take my mind off the missing Ian and off Mrs Harrison and her New Guinea nursing days and her matter-of-fact attitude to the glass slipper. Tough old bird, but soft on a Labrador called Bovver. I worked the next three days like I have never worked before. The paneling was sorted and the charcoal kiln prepped for the next load. I even loaded the feed with fresh logs. The boss was going to be surprised when he got back and got his head sorted out. I never would have guessed he was so keen on his foreman. Life is full of surprises, isn't it. After three days of working up a storm I had run out of things to do. Time for the old nap, I thought.

I hung up my leather apron and wandered around the back of the stack and nodded hello to Fred and Arthur, both perched on a couple of planks and eating their lunch. The chair sat off to one side, alone, with an abandoned air. I took an old turpentine rag and wiped it down. The blood stain was still there but it was no longer tacky and adhesive but hard and firm, like resin. Just to be on the safe side I spread an old piece of sacking over it and sat down. It was as comfortable as I remembered it. I sank back and relaxed, put my feet up and knocked my cap down over my eyes.

The leather seemed to sigh in pleasure and I felt like I sank in a little further, the chair going out of its way to make me comfortable. This was going to be a long nap.

Revenge

Dylan Dunkley

A S I WALKED down the highway I could only think of that bastard that killed my mum. I was heading straight ahead, didn't know where, all I knew was I was heading the same way as his red Holden ute. I wasn't out to forgive or forget. I was out to kill, to get my revenge.

Ten years later...

My name is Phillip Martinez. I'm thirty four years old. I have no house, no job, and no life. I am on the way to killing a man they call Donald Hosgan. I have been after him for ten years and have received two gunshot wounds from men that work for him. One in the right shoulder and the other in the right leg.

Hosgan has killed eleven people in the last ten years, one of whom was my mother. I'm out to get revenge.

On the left of me is Joshua Ridges, or as we call him, Sparky. He is our technical expert. On my right is David Sherogan. He is our sharpshooter. He was a sniper in the army for seven years. Behind us are thirty other people who are either friends or family of people that Hosgan has killed. We are all on the lookout for Hosgan and will keep looking for as long as it takes us.

We continue walking down the abandoned road through the town.

As we walk along we spot a red Holden ute. David, with his gun raised, was already running up to the parked ute. He snuck around the side and peeked through the windows. He saw nothing but a box full of what looked like books. By this time everyone was spread out around the car park. Hiding behind other cars and buildings. All waiting. David, Sparky and I ran behind a brick wall about two hundred metres away. We sat waiting for forty seven minutes until we finally saw a man walking towards the car. I raised my gun, aiming it at him. When the man's face came out of the shadows we saw it wasn't him. I let out a long depressing sigh. Again it was the wrong man.

Then David tapped me on the shoulder and signalled me to look. There was another man coming out of the shadows. As his face was shown we noticed it was Donald Hosgan.

"Finally," I thought. I signaled for everyone to begin fire but nothing happened. I turned around and noticed that everyone except Sparky, David and me were dead. Lying on the cold concrete swimming in their own blood. When I turned back to look at Donald he was standing in front of me with a gun pointing at my head. I knew it was the end for me.

Our Kokoda

Bruce Lyman

Who are you that disturbs this track?
Who plods, head down
Under weight of pack?
Who disturbs my rest, my sleep?

Who walks my highway of dreams?
Who are you who claims to know
Villages and hills you can't pronounce,
And sleeps on graves unknown, unnamed?

You tell them you come to test your legs.
You whisper you come to test your heart.
Yet you stagger, with no breakfast
And stop before the sun goes down.

Who are you who begrudges the rain
And moans when fancy boots get wet?
Who are you under Gortex dome,
Armed with antibiotics in your pack?

Who is the God you walk with?
Carve his name on your heart, lest
It is shot through without warning
By copper jacketed metal, Nippon cast.

Who are you who pretends to know this jungle scar?
Your knees complain and shoulders ache
And you take home a certificate
That says "Conquered".

I hear your clumping boots and scuffing step
And I thank the Lord for your sake I am not a Jap.
I hear you mangle place names, and your cry,
"My kingdom for water, just a sip."

I roll over at your moaning – a blister
I hate the sound of your complaint.
I see you walk without seeing
And wonder at your heart.

I follow you into Kokoda.
I see you slip your pack.
My own with ammo and mortar still binds me,
But now I glimpse your heart.

You are a Joe like me, both from unchaste loins.
Both called from ordinary places.
Only I do things that become ordinary,
To kill, no less and be killed – again and again.

You are a walker like me. None of us are
Born to kill. We are both walkers on a mission.
You are a walker, still living
Not lost 'neath this leaf and fungus.

Keep walking you disturber of my sleep
Keep your head down if you must, but think.

Close your eyes if you have to, and do not look
Lest my blood and my enemy offend.

For today you can walk with your Gortex
And pills and hot food and sat phones and
Emergency airlift because I carved this track
Beneath you with my heart.

Just don't forget me under this forest
And peat. My helmet is gone,
Rusted away, but my blood is the mud
Clinging to your boots.

Disturb my sleep my brother
Walk where I walked and talk to God.
Walk where I walked and weep in your heart
For the dead here for you, 'neath this sod.

Port Moresby, October 2010

A New Story

Ellen Cregan

I MAGINE A WORLD where owning or reading a book was against the law. Well, welcome to my life. My name is Josh and I live in a small town called Nina. It's just on the edge of North America. Just yesterday books were banned. It was a pretty silly reason. What happened was...

The whole town was called to the Town Hall to hear some old lady complain because her son was reading Harry Potter and then he started acting like a wizard. Then he thought he could make his homework be magically done. So the foolish kid didn't do any and got an F in math and in grammar. See, a very silly reason.

So, then books were banned and I was bored out of my mind and had no idea what to do. I asked Mum but as always she has the worst ideas...

"Mum I'm bored," I complained.

"Well you should think of something to do, something creative."

"Like what?"

"Oh, here is a good idea. Why don't you host a barbecue. Wouldn't that be fun?"

You can probably guess what I said next. "But mum I don't…"

"I know you don't want to but at least think about it; it would be something to do. You could invite Ben and he's bound to be better by the time you finish, so just think about it okay."

"But mum." Then she gave me the look so I gave up.

"Okay I'll think about it. I'm going to bed. Goodnight, see you in the morning."

I leaned up and kissed her on the right cheek then ran down the hallway to my bed before she could say goodnight, although I thought I heard her call out "Goodnight darling" after me.

When I got to my room I pulled some clean pyjamas from my draw and brushed my teeth. Why do I have to brush my teeth when I'm only going to eat breakfast in the morning and then brush them after? Oh well. When I was done I jumped into bed and curled up into a ball and started to think of how much the world needs books. Without books there is no imagination, nothing you can look forward to like, what is going to happen next? Now I know that if you are reading this you probably have something different. Maybe in the future there is a box that has moving pictures on it. Ha, now I'd like to see that one. So I uncurled and sat on my bed for half an hour and decided on a plan. My plan was to get books back but I would have to do it without Mum knowing. So I'll do the barbecue to keep her happy. I'll start my plan in the morning.

I woke up really early so that I could have some time with my plan. I worked hard until Mum got up then I got back into bed and pretended to be asleep. When mum came in I pretended to wake up (I am very good). I gave out a big yawn. "Morning Mum."

"Morning darling. I'll just put on some porridge. Would you like honey or sugar on your porridge?"

"Umm, I'll just have sugar today," I replied. Then I got back to work on my plan for a bit, keeping in mind that I had to also plan a barbecue as well. I worked out that if I write a book that is really good and has nothing you can copy, and you can do nothing after reading it except to write more and more books then that would convince them that not all books were bad. It was a good plan but it will take a while to get heaps of books back because the mayor burned all books to make sure no one can read or own a book. As I was going through my plan I realised how important books were to a normal kid. Even though the kids say they hate books and wish they were gone, when they get their wish they realise how much they don't hate them and how much they need them in their lives. And that is when I decided to write about a world where owning or reading a book was against the law.

"Breakfast is ready!" shouted Mum from down the hall.

"Coming!"

I folded up my piece of paper and walked quickly down the hall. When I got there I sat down in my seat and poured milk on my porridge. I tried to eat my porridge as quick as I could without Mum noticing.

"Your Dad called today. He is coming home in a week," she said as she sat down at the table.

"That's good," I said as I took another spoonful of porridge.

The porridge burned my mouth but I kept eating so I would be finished sooner. When I got back to my room to write some more I realised how much I had written and that all I had to do was write a conclusion, and I know that when you write a story that it usually takes days or months or years, but it all seemed to flow together so well that I couldn't stop. The conclusion wasn't that hard but for some reason I didn't want to stop. I wanted more time but I knew that the sooner it was done the sooner books would be back.

So I kept on writing and in an hour I was done. Now all I had to think about was a way to get it to the mayor. Maybe I could volunteer to go get groceries for my barbecue. Perfect! I put all the pages in a neat pile and put it in my backpack and walked to the lounge where Mum was comfortably sitting in front of the fire. I bet if all books were allowed she'd be reading one.

"Hey Mum," I said as I sat down on the couch next to her.

"I've decided to host that barbecue so I'm just going to go down to the supermarket to see how much everything is".

"That's great," she said, sounding surprised.

"I'll be back by lunchtime," I said as I got up from the couch.

Then I gave her a hug and ran out the door, jumped on my bike and pedalled as fast as I could down the winding street. The sooner I got there the sooner this nightmare would be over.

It took fifteen minutes to get to the Town Hall. When I arrived I parked my bike right outside the small grey building. I held onto my backpack straps as I climbed the five steps leading to the front door. Knock, knock. It didn't take very long for someone to get to the door.

"So organised," I mumbled to myself.

"Hello, can I help you?" the man at the door said.

"Umm, yes, I am here to see the mayor." I stumbled to find the words.

"Ah yes," he said as he glared at my backpack. "Come in."

I slowly walked in, looking around at the beautifully painted white walls and the pictures. I followed the strange man down a hallway to a big brown door at the end of it.

"This better be good. But I guess it doesn't matter, the mayor is always happy to receive visitors. After all he does not get many these days," he said as he opened the door.

"Ah, welcome!" the mayor shouted from behind his desk. "What do we have here?" he asked in excitement.

"Hi, my name is Josh and I think that you should have books brought back to this town. I know that all the books were banned because they had a bad influence on people so I wrote my own and…" I choked out too quickly.

"Wait a minute. Did you just say you wrote your own book?" he asked with a look of surprise.

"Well yes, it's really good and the only thing it influences you to do is write and read more books." I was getting more confident as I went on.

"I'll take a look at it and get back to you soon. Just leave your number here."

"Okay, thank-you. Bye," I said when I had finished writing down my number.

"Talk to you soon," he said as I walked out the door.

I got on my bike and headed to the store. When I got there I found it was closed. So I headed back home to wait for a call. When I got home Mum was making lunch.

"You're back early," Mum noticed.

"The shops were closed so I'll go down tomorrow."

"In that case you can help me make lunch."

"Okay, I guess I can," I agreed.

When we had finished making lunch we sat down and began to eat. I was halfway into my sandwich when the phone rang. I ran to pick it up.

"Hello this is Josh speaking."

"Hello Josh, this is the mayor. I've read your story and it has touched me and I have decided to bring books back to the town. I have also decided to publish your book as the first book. You should be very proud." I nearly shouted out loud when I heard the news.

"That's great!" I said, trying to not sound too loud.

"The town meeting will be held tomorrow at nine o'clock. Hope to see you there," he said.

"Okay, I will see you then. Bye."

He hung up.

"Who was that?" Mum asked when I put down the phone.

"Mum," I started to say.

"Yes?" she pushed.

I decided to tell her the truth.

"I am bringing books back to this town by writing my own story and giving it to the mayor to prove that not all books have a bad influence in them. So when I said I was going to get the price of things I needed I was really presenting my story to the mayor."

Mum quickly shut her open mouth. "You wrote a book?"

"Yeah, and the mayor's going to have a meeting with everyone and publish it as the first book ever written."

"Okay, well when is this meeting then?" she asked in a sarcastic tone.

"It's going to be at the Town Hall at nine o'clock tomorrow and the whole town is going to be there!" I said, now really excited.

"Wait a minute, are you telling me the truth?" she asked, her mouth open again.

"Yes, the whole thing is the truth," I said, a bit too loud.

"Well that's great!"

She walked over to me and well, I'm not sure how hard she was squeezing me but I couldn't breathe.

"Mum – can't – breathe." She let go and I let in a gasp of air.

"Sorry. Are you still going to have a barbecue?" she asked with open eyes.

"Umm, yes but it will have a theme of 'Books'."

"That sounds great!" she shouted.

For the rest of the day I worked on my speech. It didn't have to be very long which was good and when it was finally time I was more prepared than ever. So I gave my speech and my book was published as the first book ever written in the town and books were brought back. My life went from boring to even more boring to the life that everyone envies. I know it is not good to envy people but I help them in writing their own books all the time and if I ask my secret I tell them... If you get stuck, keep going. If no one is there to support you, keep going. And even when your life feels like it is going nowhere and you feel like there is nothing to motivate you, KEEP GOING.

About the Authors

Mary Arch

Mary is thankful that she lives in a culture and a time that allows her to read and write. She was born in Adelaide and grew up in South East Asia. After studying literature and education at university, she went on to teach primary and secondary school for about 12 years. Mary has relished words and language since she was very young and has recently revived her love of creative writing. She is an avid reader and cannot go a day without reading a good book. Mary's other favourite pastimes are long walks and running. Much of her inspiration for writing comes when she's treading the pavement. She now lives in Brisbane.

Stephen Chan

It is Stephen's research work in muscle tissue (which uses mice as guinea pigs - there has to be a story in that) which led to the naming of our group "Fast Twitch." Also part of the original brainstorming of the group into existence Steve, when immersed in his lab work at the University of NSW, dreams of becoming a world famous author.

Ellen Cregan

Ellen is a student at Northern Beaches Christian School in Grade 10. She loves creative writing and has been crafting stories ever since she could get crayons onto the wallpaper. She can't remember the name of her favourite author but she aspires to be a well known writer just like ah, ah,... . Gemma Malley! If she could have anything published other than what is in this volume it would be the Elf story she started writing when she was in Grade 4. It has not progressed past 3 pages.

Gordon Crossin

Gordon works for our government in all sorts of exotic places and gets to travel a bit. He also gets given cam uniforms to wear. Currently living in the Northern Territory, Gordon can boast being our most distant contributor.

Chris Dunkley

Chris finished he final year of high school last year and is now looking around at his options. As are a few others on his behalf as well. He errs on the side of crafting fantasy tales and is remarkably prolific once the pen starts to roll – and it takes so very little to get him going. His ideal is to illustrate his own writing.

Dylan Dunkley

On the contrary it takes this writer a while to get wound up but once moving proves to be very creative. Dylan enjoys developing his characters though in equal measure enjoys killing them off in dramatic and bloody ways. He is really a closet writer of romance.

Sonja Goernitz

Sonja is an Author, Journalist and Researcher from Hamburg, now living in Sydney. She came to Australia for the first time in July 1998 and has travelled, worked and studied here. She received Permanent Residency in 2005. Initially she met Australians in California. They were nice people – but were not impressed by the beaches. So she thought: Australia must be a great place...

Michael Henderson

Michael Henderson is a try hard storyteller working in the areas of art, literature and film. He lives in Sydney, Australia, and loves his family, art, motor-sport, golf, how Jesus can transform lives, and coffee.

Bruce Lyman

Bruce has been an idle scribbler for too many years but has recently been paying more attention to getting his writing finished off and published. He enjoys travelling and his stories tend to be rooted in the experiences of meeting new people in obscure situations. Resident in Sydney he works for an humanitarian aid agency which keeps him pretty much distracted from all the writing he really wants to do.

Greg Sampson

Greg's creative writing talent is hidden by all the sales and marketing material that consumes his day to day life. Nonetheless we have been able to lure him out with the writing contained in here and are really looking forward to seeing more.

Matt White

Matt is a storeman whose brainstorming contributed to the first piece of writing for the group – Killer Forklifts. Matt almost never puts pen to paper – his pieces are written on his cell phone and emailed for later editing. Not the usual approach but it works and he at least has no ink stains on his fingers.

www.ingramcontent.com/pod-product-compliance
Lightning Source LLC
Chambersburg PA
CBHW052148170626

46812CB00004B/1634